Dog Park Romeo

By
M K Scott

Books by M K Scott

The Talking Dog Detective Agency
Cozy Mystery
A Bark in the Night
Requiem for a Rescue Dog Queen
Bark Twice for Danger
The Ghostly Howl
Dog Park Romeo

The Painted Lady Inn Mysteries Series
Culinary Cozy Mystery
Murder Mansion
Drop Dead Handsome
Killer Review
Christmas Calamity
Death Pledges a Sorority
Caribbean Catastrophe
Weddings Can be Murder
The Skeleton Wore Diamonds
Death of a Honeymoon
Cakewalk to Murder (March 2019)

The Way Over the Hill Gang Series
Cozy Mystery
Late for Dinner
Late for Bingo
Late for Shuffleboard (June 2019)

Chapter One

THE CLOUDS MOVED aside allowing the sun to shine briefly on the icicle-laden buildings and the dirty snow piled up in the parking lot. People bundled up in thick coats hurried to the businesses, all except two women accompanied by a large black dog. They strolled casually to a restaurant while talking.

The first woman glanced up at the sky and shook her head. "Winter lasts forever or it seems to. In Indiana, all you have are cold, gray days that stretch into infinity, especially after the Christmas rush is over. Decorated trees started showing up in stores in October, and the radio stations started playing 'The Little Drummer Boy' before it was even Thanksgiving. Don't get me started on all those holiday romance movies and now *this*."

Her arm stretched out indicating businesses bare of holiday decorations and only sporting a few icicles, which, located right over their door, had the tendency to drip a freezing drop whenever someone entered or exited.

"Karly," Nala prompted, seizing an opening. She knew good and well her best friend was avoiding her earlier question. "Speaking of romance, whatever happened to you and Harry? You two were inseparable after Comic Con."

"Oh, that didn't work out." She sighed a little, then said, "Happiness is a journey, not a destination."

Nala stopped, pulling her dog to a stop as she did so. He sported a harness with an aluminum handle better suited for a blind person. She slipped on a pair of dark glasses to match the image. "Oh please. Everyone who says happiness is a journey is already where they want to be. Sure, it's easy to say it's not about the goal when you're sitting in some big bucks mansion or starring on a hit television show."

"It *could* be about the journey."

"Give me a break." She pushed up the slipping dark glasses. "I hate doing this, but you know in the winter months there's no outside dining, and most restaurants aren't accepting about dogs inside."

"Yeah, what's up with that?" asked the dog in question. Max, the handsome, black shepherd mix could speak, but would not bark on command for some reason. Instead, he could speak in English, courtesy of a disgruntled girlfriend—who happened to be a witch— of his first owner. Despite all the movies and children's books about talking dogs, most people weren't cool about it.

"Not now, Max. We're talking about Harry," Nala reminded both her dog and her best friend.

"Let's just say it was fun while it lasted, but it's over now."

"Really? That's it?" She stumbled as they approached the entrance of the restaurant. "These glasses are too dark. I hope this works"

Karly reached out to cup her friend's elbow when Max spoke. "Leading her is *my* job. You, the one with hands, can open the door."

Instead, a few diners leaving pushed open the door, releasing the smell of barbecued meat and onions, which caused Max to moan. "I expect some quality meat thrown under the table."

The exiting diners murmured among themselves, probably commenting on the deep voice that either she or Karly had. It became apparent—shortly after she rescued Max from the dog shelter where her best friend worked—that people don't believe in talking dogs. She'd just come off sounding crazy if she mentioned the subject. It was probably best not to. Many would take advantage of the situation.

"Step up," Karly instructed. "I'm surprised your guide dog didn't make you aware of the threshold."

The comment made Max surge forward, almost tripping her. She managed to regain her balance and made it into the restaurant where the hostess asked if they wanted a handicapped table. Nala wasn't even sure what that meant. Was the table different somehow? "No, a large booth will do."

They made it to the booth without any mishaps. The waitress hurried off to find the one braille menu they had, giving Max time to settle underneath the table. Nala pulled the glasses down enough to take in the booth before sliding into it. "I'm not sure how anyone sees anything with these glasses on."

Karly laughed and coughed. "Think about it."

"Yeah, I know. As soon as I said it, I realized the obvious. By the way, I want the chicken barbecue sandwich with sweet potato fries. Oh, and an iced tea to drink." Max shoved her leg with his heavy body. "Add a Texas Brisket with no sauce and steak fries."

Her friend chuckled. "Good luck getting him to eat kibble after brisket."

"Tell me about it."

The server showed up with glasses of water. She placed one in front of Nala and told her it was there. Nala had to suppress saying anything since the action was a courtesy for a sight-impaired customer.

Karly remembered to ask for a pan of water for Max.

"Thanks, bestie. Max will be thirsty after wolfing down all the smoked meat. So, tell me what went wrong with Harry. He seemed like a nice guy to me."

"Me, too," Max commented from under the table.

Nala nudged her chatty pet with the toe of her boot but had already learned he often spoke at inappropriate times and refused to speak when she wanted him to—like the time she was trying to convince her mother she didn't have a man hidden in her office after hearing Max's voice on the intercom.

"He *is* a nice guy." A wistful expression conveyed her thoughts on the man. "He's sweet, kind, and well, a doofus. All the things I like in a male."

"What's the issue?" It didn't make sense her friend would throw away a perfectly acceptable man, especially since she'd been on the hunt so long.

"It might just be me," Karly stated. "I don't trust a man who doesn't own a dog or any kind of pet for that matter."

She understood her friend's huge love for dogs. Why else would she work at the shelter when she could make much more money elsewhere? "You don't own a dog."

"I want to, but my apartment won't let me. I've saved Boston, the terrier mix, countless times by falsifying his date of entry. I eventually got him into a breed specific rescue group. That's my go-to when I can't get an animal adopted. You know I love animals. It's hard to love a man who doesn't love them, too."

"I think you're making a snap judgment. Harry keeps dog treats in his office for Max. That's not the action of a dog-hating individual."

From underneath the table, Max added. "He's the man. Good treats, too. None of that cheap stuff that's too salty and hard."

"He never told me about the dog treats." Her fingers went up to rub her temples. "Maybe I was too hasty."

Nala nodded—not that she had room to criticize after her treatment of Officer Tyler Goodnight. The handsome veteran turned cop still made appearances in her daydreams and the occasional night dream. "Did you tell him why you didn't want to see him?"

"Of course not. I was just busy. Eventually, Harry stopped calling as much. It's been at least a couple of weeks since I've heard from him."

"The slow fade. I can't believe it. You were never a fan when it was used on *you*." Even though Nala had never been a big fan of her friend's previous boyfriends, she disliked how they left the scene even more. Usually, they forgot to return texts, phone calls, etc. One even hid behind a locked door when Karly showed up to see if he was okay after he updated his social status to dead.

"That's why I never mentioned it. I knew you would become all fussy and judgy on me."

Before she could bristle at the label, an employee arrived with the food, causing Max to lurch up and hit his head on the table. "Ouch!"

"Oh, did I burn you?" the server asked in horror. "I didn't mean to. That last thing I'd ever want to do is hurt a blind person. I figure you've got enough problems making it through your day to day life. You'll never be able to enjoy a movie in those lounger seats."

Nala held up her hand to stop the ramble. "Please. I'm okay. No worries."

When the server left, she picked up a slice of brisket and moved it under the table where Max gently took it from her fingers.

Karly stirred sweetener into her glass of tea. "I'm glad you stopped the man before he listed everything you couldn't do as a sight-impaired person. You know Jenny, who works at the shelter, is legally blind. She still goes to the movies. She gets these special headphones that tell her what's going on when the characters aren't speaking. So, he's wrong about the movie part."

"I figured as much. I could have left Max behind, but I have a case that might be right up your alley. Remember how you were always begging to help me? Most of the time, I don't have enough work for two people. Since Sawyer started working with me, he helps me out whenever I don't need a specific gender for undercover work."

Karly stuck her tongue out at her, letting her know her feelings about that.

"I could see that. My eyes must be adapting to the glasses. Anyhow, this new case, or I should say *cases,* should be golden, or at least, just right for you." She stopped to take a bite of her sandwich before it got cold. The sweet and tangy barbecue sauce was exactly as she remembered.

Using a fry as a prop, Karly waved it in Nala's direction. "You're going to do that, tell me how something is perfect for me, then stop?"

"Eating," she managed between bites. She took a handful of steak fries and put them beside her on the vinyl seat where Max could take them at his leisure. They vanished immediately. Leisure was never a word Max used with food. As a dog who had been out on the streets, she should expect as much.

Karly popped the fry into her mouth and chewed. She still managed to convey annoyance with lowered brows and a wrinkled nose.

Making her friend wait was mean of her. Brownies! She reverted to one of her cookie curses her father had encouraged her to use when she was caught as a pre-teen using a not so sugary word. The habit had stuck, which made it difficult to convince clients she was a hard-boiled private eye. Sometimes, she enjoyed teasing her friend, who could be a little over dramatic. Not too much or she would be as bad as Elvin, her subcontractor and friend who was never above pulling a practical joke. He was the one who got the harness and service dog vest for Max.

At the time, he had been dog-sitting while Nala and Karly went on a wine tour. His goal was to solicit sympathy from women he assumed would feel sorry for a blind guy. Instead, he was tossed out of the bar by the boyfriend of the woman he'd been flirting with. He later gave the supplies to Nala, thinking she could make better use of them.

The possibility of her acting like Elvin had her swallowing in a hurry to speak. "Okay, I've had two clients come to me about a man they met at the dog park."

Her friend's shoulders went up in a shrug. "Not surprising. Men try to meet women at the dog park all the time. I've even had men come into the shelter and ask me what breed attracts the most babes.

I was always leery about letting them adopt. My fellow employees, not as much. Usually, those dogs left on Friday and came back on a Monday because they didn't work the expected magic. No dog can make up for a creepy owner. I imagined those guys were hustlers, offering to walk their dogs or something."

"No." She wiped at a dribble of barbecue sauce before continuing. "Lois, my first client, claimed he was charming—a handsome fellow who called himself Allan. He had a gorgeous golden retriever."

"How is this a problem? I've been to the park a lot with rescue dogs, and I've never had a guy flirt with me."

"You're probably better off. This guy asks for money on the first date and never asks for a second."

"Huh? You mean he's asking women for money at the park? That would be a turn-off for me. What's the deal?"

That was indeed the question. She exhaled audibly. "At this point, I don't know. Lois told me she went out with Allan, and the date went well until the end when the man started crying."

"That has never happened to me, and if it did, I would not throw money at the guy. I'd excuse myself to the restroom and hope he got it back together before I returned after a reasonable length of time. What's the deal?"

Many women wouldn't return to the table, but her tender-hearted friend would. Lois had to be cut from the same cloth. "He told Lois his dog had heartworms and had to undergo the treatment, but he had just lost his job and couldn't afford the thousand dollars. Lois fell for it and gave him the money."

The grimace said more about Karly's feeling about the tale than the tenderloin she was consuming, which Nala knew to be extraordinary, pretty much like everything on the menu. "Yeah, I thought it sounded suspicious, too. Why would you ask someone out when you couldn't even afford your own dog's medical treatment?"

Karly slapped the table. "That's dirty, but at least his dog will get treatment. It's better than those who surrender their dogs to the shelter due to medical expenses. They don't want to hear the low-cost options they could use, either."

Her friend had missed the point, which Nala had been afraid of. "I don't think his dog *had* heartworms. She told me the dog ran everywhere, just like a dog food commercial, with no obvious signs of being winded."

"That *does* sound suspicious. Why didn't she think of that before she gave him the money?"

"He was sobbing in a public restaurant."

"I can see that as being a problem, but later on she must have realized she'd been had."

"That's when she came to me, and she's not the only one."

Max's head settled on her lap as if to question why the food had stopped. Nala surveyed the area but halted when she realized a blind woman wouldn't. She slipped the brisket plate under the table, which kept her dog busy.

"Is Allan trying this on all the dog park ladies? Don't they actually talk when their dogs are playing?" Karly asked.

It would be logical for people to talk, but Nala had stood in plenty of lines, elevators, and even buses were people pretended not to notice the person crammed next to them. "It would be helpful if they did. The next lady, Madeline, described her dog park Romeo as looking like a young Mark Harmon."

"Who?"

"That guy on NCIS."

"The cute Hispanic dude?"

"No, the other one that doesn't talk much."

"He's old."

"She did say a younger version. Besides, none of my clients are young. They're close to my mother's age. Anyhow, he had a French Bulldog with cancer. It was going to cost eight thousand dollars to help poor Bobo."

"Let me guess." Karly made a face. "The woman gave it to him and never heard from him again?"

"She didn't have eight thousand dollars, but she was willing to start the treatment and asked for the name of the animal hospital. Edward, which is the name he used, gave her the name of the animal hospital and their PayPal address."

"That sounds legit."

"Of course, only she could never get in contact with him again. I visited the animal hospital, and they knew nothing about Bobo or his owner. As for the PayPal address, they don't have one. The receptionist joked about them being really old school."

With an obvious follow up to her statement, she waited for her friend to ask about the PayPal address. Instead, Karly placed a hand over her heart. "What type of con artist uses innocent dogs to perpetuate a crime? Let's go get him or possibly *them*. I'm all in."

Chapter Two

IT WAS ONLY ten in the morning on a Saturday. Inside the fence, the cordoned off dog area from the regular park looked like an outdoor party with dogs. The owners were bundled up in puffy jackets and caps. A few were willing to brave the elements in only a sports team sweatshirt or a ski sweater. They were the ones usually running with their dog as if training for the Olympics.

Nala shook her head from her position near a large oak tree. *Show-offs.* That's what those who were running were doing.

Broad Ripple was fortunate to have a dog park, but it wasn't huge. If a person wanted to run, there were other entire parks to do that in. Nope, not these guys. These guys wanted to be seen by the women clutching coffee cups in their gloved hands. Where was Karly anyway?

The plan was for her to show up with a shelter dog and pretend to be a doting dog lover, which wouldn't be much of an act for her friend. A car door slammed, and a frenzied spate of barking had a conversing dog owner turning to see what owner couldn't keep control of his or her animal. A large, white dog lunged toward the dog park, pulling Karly behind him. Her friend had on stiletto heel boots that had to be hard to walk in, let alone run in, as she was presently doing.

Inside the dog park, people rushed about snapping on leads and cutting their time short as they hurried their canines to their respective cars. Nala watched the scene in horror as one owner picked up her small, fluffy dog and raced to her vehicle. This wasn't working out as she planned.

Nala came out from her hiding place and greeted Karly. "Hello, you're late. Couldn't you have brought a little less energetic dog? You'll clean the place out." She blinked when she caught a good look at her friend. Here she'd thought the boots were ridiculous. "Are you wearing false eyelashes?"

"That's what took so long and the fact we had no adoptable dogs."

Max, who had been hiding, came out from behind a tree. "What's that? I would have thought it was a dog, but I have been wrong at least once or even twice in the past."

"Diesel." Karly smiled when she said the name. "He's a newbie. His owners just surrendered him. They're having a baby and didn't think they could have him along with a baby."

"Why's that?" Max asked. "Children love dogs."

Despite Max ending up in a shelter, he still hadn't learned that people often lie about their motivations for ridding themselves of a dog. "Some children love dogs," Nala conceded. "Others are terrified of them."

The decoy dog ignored Max as he sniffed each inch of the park, pulling Karly behind him. "Children who aren't raised with dogs are terrified of them. I told the man as much, too. It didn't change his mind."

"Could be his dog has no manners," Nala suggested, well aware that was no excuse to dump a dog at the shelter.

"Diesel's just excited to be outside." The words trailed off as Karly reluctantly followed the dog.

Why did most of her undercover assignments turn out like this? None of them went smoothly like those on television. On the positive side, she usually wasn't being shot at, which was a plus. Her gaze dropped to Max. "Can't you talk to him and tell him to calm down or something?"

His lips lifted as he was attempting to smirk but failed. "I can try. Remember, you didn't have much luck influencing preschoolers, and they're your own kind."

Leave it to her to take home the smart-aleck rescue pooch. She rolled her eyes. Unfortunately, Max had hit the nail on the head. She left teaching preschool since she felt she made such little impact. Any organization or discipline she tried to instill was undone by indulgent parents. "Just try, please."

Instead of answering, Max loped after the fast disappearing Karly and Diesel. He barked as he ran, sharp, commanding sounds that punched holes in the air. If she didn't know Max as well as she did, it would be frightening to have a large dog running and barking at her. With any luck, Diesel might feel the same and stop or possibly run for his life, dragging Karly behind him. Snickerdoodles! What had she done?

She broke into a run, spotting the three outside the dog park. Max's confident bark sounded a little less strident as he herded the other dog back into the park enclosure. Sometimes, she forgot about Max's ancestry, until he did something that proved he was more than a wise-cracking canine. As they moved closer, she could hear Karly complaining.

"Slower, Max. I about twisted my ankle a dozen times already in these boots."

Her friend's words made her smile a little, and she strolled over to meet them. "Let's get Diesel back to the center. We can head over to your place where you can change into something that won't cause you to break any limbs, and we can discuss our game plan."

"Roger that," Karly agreed with a sigh. "Not sure if I am cut out to be undercover."

"Not in those boots, for sure. Not your style. Where did you get them?"

The dog in question sat without being asked, then laid down as if tired. Nala smiled at Max. "You worked some magic there, bud."

"All in a day's work, ma'am." He gave a nod of his dark, elegantly shaped head.

It was hard to know if the quote was from the westerns Max enjoyed or from the vintage cop shows her father favored. "You did good, and I owe you a—"

"A cheeseburger," he finished for her.

"You'll get it." She turned her attention to Karly. "What's the getup for?"

"I wanted to look like I was open for some male attention."

Nala laughed. It was hard to know what else to do. Her friend wanted to help with undercover work so much. "Ah well, you went overboard. I guess I should have given you a heads up. My assumption was you'd wear your normal clothes. Jeans and your zip-up hoodie that has the assorted dog silhouettes on it. Maybe a beanie due to the chill in the air."

"If I did that, I would look like everyone else in the park." She shook her head. "I needed to stand out."

"Oh, you stood out, all right. Luckily, since the dog owners scattered so quickly, I doubt anyone noticed you. Even if they did, I'd doubt they'd recognized you with your over the top fake eyelashes and sparkly headband. You'd fit right in one of those toddler pageants with the amount of makeup you have on. Let's take Diesel back. It will take a great deal of work before he can safely make it back to the dog park."

Karly handed the lead to Nala, then hobbled over to a bench and sat. "These boots have to go. They're going to cripple me. It's no wonder they sat around in the center's lost and found for two months with no one ever claiming them. The poor sucker who was wearing them must have stripped them off and walked out of the place barefoot. I have a good mind to do the same, but at least I have socks on."

She removed the boots with a flourish, then stood and carried the offending footwear to a trash container. "Good riddance." She tossed them in and grinned. "I'm ready. Let's go."

A much calmer Diesel walked between Nala and Max. Maybe he'd only been excited to get out.

Looking at the ground littered with decaying leaves and odd patches of snow, Nala said, "I'm not so sure you should be walking without shoes. It's probably below freezing."

"I'm tough, and I have shoes in the car. No worries."

"If you say so." It wasn't unusual for Karly to put on a strong front. She joked she had to do it to protect her soft marshmallow center. "Just watch where you—"

"Ooh," Her friend grimaced and held one foot up gingerly. "Well, I can't say that's my first experience doing that. The good news is I brought along plastic bags for such an occasion. Good thing I have extra clothes at the center, too."

"I'll follow you, or I can swing by, get lunch, and take it to your apartment."

Before Karly could answer, Max did. "Cheeseburgers! Let's go get them."

They reached the parking lot. Karly headed to her car, and when she reached it, she leaned against it to peel off the offending sock. "If everyone scooped their dog poop, this wouldn't have happened."

"You're so right. If everyone behaved in a decent fashion, doing exactly what they were supposed to do, you and I would be out of work."

"True." Karly opened up the back door of her car and motioned for Diesel to enter. Unlike his earlier exuberant self, the large dog stepped into the car without a sound.

"I'll see you at the apartment." Nala held up her hand and waited for her friend to wave back before she made her way to her vintage beetle.

Max jumped in and took the shotgun seat as he usually did. Nala climbed in after him and had just started the car when her mobile chimed. The caller identification showed it was Officer Tyler Goodnight. What could he possibly want?

Chapter Three

NALA STARED AT the phone in her hand. If she let it ring one more time it would go to voice mail. She might not have spent much time with the man, but she did know he wasn't a big fan of voice mail. Good chance he'd hang up without a message, and she'd never know why he called. In the middle of its final ring, she picked up.

"Hello?" She hated that her voice was so breathy.

"Ah, hi, it's me, Tyler."

"I know. Your name came up."

"Oh." His voice swung up indicating interest. "You still have my number in your phone."

That made her sound bad, as if she was still hanging out and hoping he might call. Maybe she had been doing exactly that. It just seemed like the desire was there to get together, but whenever they did, something happened, like his old girlfriend showing up.

"I have a lot of numbers in my phone. As a private investigator, I regard you as an excellent resource."

"Resource, huh? I bet your father would be a better one. He has higher clearance than I do."

He made a valid point, which would make it hard for her to sound so offhand about everything. She wanted to sound like she didn't care, when she did. It was important for him to think she never thought about him, more than she'd like to admit.

"Yeah, but sometimes I just want an answer. Often, if I ask my father a question, he ends up taking over. You know how he is."

"I do." He cleared his throat and rushed to clarify his answer. "I mean, he's the best at getting things done."

"Come on. You don't have to do that. I'm not reporting to my father, and even he knows he can be a little overwhelming. There's his way, the wrong way, and the highway."

"Yep. I may have heard that one at the academy."

"I bet you did. So, why did you call? I know it wasn't to talk about my father."

He gave a short, forced laugh. "I'm calling for a friend."

This was how fifty-percent of her phone inquiries started out. The *I'm asking for a friend* ploy meant the person was just feeling her out and often hoped for a solution without paying for it. "What does your friend need?"

"Background check on the man she's dating."

"Hmm…" She gave a non-committal reply as she considered the possibility of Tyler really having a friend who needed private investigation services. Could this be a ruse just to talk to her? "I imagine the police could check the name easily enough."

"We did. Nothing came up. He doesn't have a criminal history. Still, Daphne thinks something isn't quite right."

"She doesn't have to date him. That's always an option."

"I told her as much."

"What do you want me to do?"

"You know. Your usual peeping into the man's credit files, past wives, jobs, etc. Follow him around. Who are his buds? Where does he spend his money? You know, that date check thing you do."

"I can do that. The usual check I do from the comfort of my office. There's no surveillance work involved. Have Daphne call me for an appointment, which makes me wonder why you're calling me."

"I thought I should. Didn't know how you might act if Daphne went in and said I recommended you."

"I would act normal. I'm always interested in a paying client. I imagine I'd even be polite." The nerve of him, thinking she'd freak out at the mention of his name. "We're not talking old girlfriend here."

"Why'd you say that?"

"Never mind." She shouldn't have mentioned it. As soon as the words were out of her mouth, she knew it was a mistake. What she wouldn't give to take it back. He probably thought she was fixated on his old girlfriend. For all she knew, he *was* still dating his old girlfriend. She wrinkled her nose, knowing better. Her father made a point of telling her Tyler wasn't, which meant her father had asked. The man had no boundaries.

"How is business going? Still subbing at your old preschool job?"

The man hadn't stayed current on her business. "Thankfully, no. I have a partner, now."

"Donovan from Minnesota?"

Brownies! There was no way he should know this. It wasn't like she made an announcement in the paper. "Are you spying on me?"

"I'm not some type of stalker who follows people around." He cleared his throat again. "I'm not saying you're a stalker because you follow people. That's your job. Your father, Captain Bonne, told me."

No wonder she was single and very much unattached. She'd have to tell Dad to stop broadcasting all her business. "Okay, I'm not a stalker, and I have a partner, which allows me not to substitute teach anymore. I'll look forward to talking to Daphne. Got to go. Bye."

She hung up and smiled. Whoever hung up first held the upper hand. The rule was originally meant for business, but she could see it applying to other areas. When she was dating Jeff—who turned out to be not as big a deal as he thought he was—her mother used to tell her that those who cared the least controlled the relationship. She was never quite sure if her mother was telling her to care less or warning her about Jeff. Typical of her family. When they weren't busy telling her what to do, they came up with cryptic sayings, which was more advice, but she had to work to figure it out before rejecting it.

Thoughts of what could have been between her and Tyler chased themselves through her mind, leaving her bemused.

Max nudged her with his nose. "Those cheeseburgers aren't going to get themselves. At the rate you're *not* going, Karly will beat us to the apartment."

"Please." She started the car, and the engine rattled to life. "I think you forget who rescued whom, the way you give orders."

Max made a snorting noise and swiveled to look out the window as the car moved. With winter hanging on, there wasn't all that much to see. It was the equivalent of the canine cold shoulder. Nala had experienced it more than once. She refused to give in this time.

They drove in silence with the only noise being the occasional horn honked or the growl of a car with a faulty muffler or no muffler at all.

When the neon fast foods signs showed up along the side of the road rather like colorful mushrooms, Max deigned to comment. "I'll forgive you. Whenever Tyler calls, you get all cranky."

"No, I don't." She denied the accusation while wondering if it *was* true.

He swung his head around to stare at her with his large, liquid eyes. "You do now. Before when he called, you'd be all happy, and you'd give me two chew bones instead of one."

Had she done that? Not the happiness. That part she remembered. The bone bit. She could have if she were feeling so happy that she'd wanted to share it. Now, since she wasn't exactly ecstatic about life, Max was lucky to get one bone. Feeling a twinge of guilt, she turned into Max's favorite burger place. The food wasn't better, but they always made a fuss over Max and sometimes added two beef patties to the plain cheeseburger, which was always for Max. Mustard wasn't good for dogs and ketchup didn't do her upholstery any favors.

The dog next to her sat up, intent on where they were. "Yippee! Can I have two cheeseburgers since you are feeling bad about how you're taking your lack of a love life out on me?"

She cut her eyes to Max. The dog had to be psychic. She thought when she first got the dog that Max sent her telepathic messages. Later on, she convinced herself it was only what she thought Max would have said. No, the dog couldn't read her mind or send telepathic messages. Sometimes, like now though, she wondered.

"Two burgers for you. One for me. One for Karly. Order of fries and another order of onion rings."

"I'd like fries, too."

"Okay. Make it two orders of fries." She pulled into the long line to the drive-thru. It would be quicker to go inside, but Max wouldn't have the opportunity to meet with his adoring public. The line moved fairly fast, showing that most of the food was premade. Getting close to lunch time, it made sense to get ready for a rush.

When they finally got to the intercom, Max decided to add onto the end of Nala's order. "I need a Big Fella burger, too, dressed."

"Okay," an employee called back. "Drive around to the window."

Nala considered trying to call the employee back to cancel the last add-on. A honk somewhere in the line got her moving. She glared into her rearview mirror, trying to figure out who honked. What business did they have honking? In no way could they know if she was finished with her order or not.

"What's with the Big Fella burger?"

"Tyler, of course. It would be rude if we all were eating when he came over if we didn't have anything for him."

Life was simple in the canine world. A single phone call and Max assumed she and Tyler were phone buddies and dinner pals again. "He only called because he has a friend who wants to use my date check services."

Normally, dogs didn't roll their eyes. Somehow Max had developed the skill and demonstrated it. "Oho, that's what you think. I'm a dog, and even *I* know better."

"Maybe." The call *did* sound borderline suspicious.

"I hate to be the one who will say I told you so when Tyler shows up, but I might." He gave a dramatic sigh.

His theatrics made her smile. "Yeah, I know how you hate to announce you were right. So much so, you do it whenever that rare occurrence happens. Besides, we're going to Karly's apartment. There's no reason Tyler would be in that neighborhood. I guess that Big Fella burger will have to go in the fridge and be my lunch tomorrow."

A single whimper sounded, making Nala feel like a giant meanie. Still, she had to maintain the upper hand in the relationship. A rescue dog who could talk, read, and apparently order things off the shopping network kept her on her toes. He should not benefit from his impulsiveness.

Their favorite attendant was working and leaned out the window to pass Max a bone. Her oversized shepherd mix stood on her leg, embedding his nails into her jeans to accept the offered treat. A smaller dog wouldn't hurt as much, but she doubted it would be able to generate a menacing presence. There were times when having Max near meant keeping threatening individuals at a distance. Maybe she would let him have the Big Fella burger after she scraped the mustard off it. Might as well. Despite Max's certainty, there was no way Tyler would casually show up.

Chapter Four

THE TABLE WAS set with holiday dishes, and the air was redolent with the smell of ham, spices, and a tang of pineapple. Nala's mother, Gwen, even had a festive apron tied over her elegant pants suit. She placed the glass dish of scalloped potatoes right next to the ham holding court in the center of the table.

Graham Bonne, her father, sat at the head of the table and chatted with his daughter as his wife arranged the table layout as if prepping for a food magazine photo shoot. "I'm glad you're able to indulge your mother on this late holiday dinner."

"No problem." Having Christmas dinner almost a month late wasn't that big of a deal. Without her parents in town, the holidays had definitely been lower key. She and Karly had enjoyed a Christmas movie marathon while eating Chinese food.

"I felt guilty leaving you alone on Christmas while we went on the Panama Canal cruise." He heaved a sigh. "Your mother and I aren't getting any younger."

Gwen placed a small platter with roasted asparagus near Graham and huffed. "Speak for yourself."

"Anyhow," her father continued, "We needed to jump on the cruise because the price was so good. Not sure when we would get another chance, either. I would have felt better about leaving you if

I'd known you had someone special to spend the time with."

Not her father, too? It was bad enough that her mother showed such a marked interest in her love life and the possibility of grandchildren in the near future. Sometimes, she wondered if those crazy women who attempted to kidnap babies from the hospital nurseries had mothers who were demanding grandchildren. If so, that explained a lot.

She cleared her throat. "I spent it with Karly. We watched movies and ate Chinese."

"That's pitiful," her mother declared, as she placed the rolls on the table and took a seat. "That's not festive."

Why hadn't anyone warned her what the talking points would be at their holiday dinner? She should have known. It's not like they varied. Her parents enjoyed talking about her, her love life, her job, and Max. Where was her dog, by the way? It wasn't like him to bypass the chance of human food. She shifted in her seat and tried to peer into the kitchen.

Not getting a reply never stopped her mother in the past, and it didn't then. "At least your father and I were listening to Christmas carols on the day."

Her father grinned. "They were played by a steel drum band while we were sipping mimosas on a sugar sand beach. Quite the change from all those years of handling domestic calls." His lips pulled down into a grimace. "Good Lord. When you work the Christmas shift, there's no peace on Earth and good will to men. Just the opposite. Yeah, I needed that trip."

This was good. Maybe she'd get a reprieve on examining her life with a magnifying glass. On more than one occasion, she had considered forgoing the Sunday family dinner. A few times, she had.

25

Still, this was the holiday meal, even it was late due to the cruise. All she had to do was turn the topic, and her father was already doing that for her. "Tell me more about the cruise."

Her mother passed the rolls and answered. "We left from the Atlantic, came back from the Pacific, went through the canal, which took forever. Lots of sea days. Beverly's husband cheats at cards. The wine was way overpriced, but we did have a handsome waiter. I took a photo of him. Let me go get my camera."

"Gwen, let it go. I know Ronaldo was single, but he's too short for Nala. Anyhow, I doubt that's his name. It's probably made up. He could be on the run from something he did in his homeland. Not a good prospect. I know you and Beverly liked him because he flattered the two of you every night to get a bigger tip."

Her mother made a derisive snort. "You'll be glad to know I slipped him an extra fifty."

"What?" her father asked with raised eyebrows.

His mock outrage didn't fool Nala. As a successful, independent businesswoman, her mother tended to do as she pleased, which wasn't news to her father. He only acted upset. Her mother expected it.

Her mother winked at her. "Bev gave him a hundred. I have no clue about the rest of the women on the cruise."

"Ha! The man should have been sporting a mask instead of that tiny excuse of a mustache." He nodded his head in Nala's direction to clue her in that his tirade was for appearance only.

"Oh please." Gwen gestured to the wine. "Graham, I need you to pour. I suspect that bar attendant with the cat eye makeup got a little extra from you, too."

"Desiree's a single mother. Has to work the cruise line because

26

there are no jobs back home. She misses her children so."

"Gullible. She saw you coming." Her mother pointed at Nala. "You serve the ham."

It took a couple of minutes to get the ham served, the wine poured, the rolls passed, and a sampling of the various side dishes. With her parents' show to watch, she almost forgot about her dog. "Where's Max?"

"Oh, you mean the hairy stand-in for my future grandchild?"

There was no way Nala was touching that. It didn't matter because her mother continued. "I fixed him a plate in the kitchen."

Her mother's house served as a template for good taste while her kitchen was practically a shrine to fine dining. Gwen Bonne never did anything mediocre. As an interior designer, the kitchen sparkled like a holiday display at Macy's—all the time. Probably because she didn't allow people in it. For some reason, Max got an invitation when almost everyone else didn't. "I hope you didn't give him too much rich food. It can have a bad effect on him."

"I know what I'm doing."

Actually, she didn't. It wasn't like Nala had a dog growing up, but arguing with her mother would do her no good. Gwen naturally assumed she was an expert on everything. Nala's only recourse would be to roll down the windows and suffer the cold as she drove home to alleviate the stench of noxious dog farts.

Possibly sensing a battle of wills in progress, her father asked, "Have any interesting cases lately?"

To most, it would sound like an innocent question. In truth, her father not only wanted to know if she had any actual clients, but wanted the chance to insert that there was still an opening at the academy for her if things were less than stellar. If she suddenly leapfrogged over a bunch of legitimate candidates who had been waiting for the call, it would be labeled nepotism. Not that she had any plans to do so. The last thing she wanted to do was to work with either of her driven parents. It wasn't that she disliked her parents. She'd decided working with them wasn't her thing.

"Yes. Apparently, there's a man hanging out at the dog park, sweet talking women out of their money."

"Really?" Her father placed a bite of scalloped potatoes in his mouth and chewed thoughtfully. Once he swallowed, he added. "I haven't heard anything about that down at the precinct."

"I doubt you would. No woman wants to admit she's been tricked by someone she's dating. I have two clients who may have been fooled by the same guy with a sad dog story and imagine there are many more out there. I really don't think the women feel they have any recourse."

"Tell me more," her father urged, waving his empty fork for emphasis.

She took a deep breath, wondering about the wisdom of doing so, but both her parents had come up with decent information in the past. They could do so again. It wasn't free or painless, though. She'd have to do something in return. Last time, she did a spa day with her mother. It sounded good in theory to anyone she told, but they weren't being questioned in detail about where her mother had gone wrong since Nala obviously despised children.

"My two clients met a man who had a dog in the park. I'm not even sure if it was the same man. This could be a new con that men are using on dog-loving females. Anyhow, the man chats up the woman. They make arrangements for a date. On the date, he mentions some horrible health problem his dog has and how he doesn't have the money to pay for it. The first woman offered to lend him the money. After she did, she heard nothing from him. No second date. On reflection, she thought his dog was pretty active for a canine on its last legs."

Her father took a bite of his roll and gestured with the remaining bread. "What about the second woman?"

"Similar story, only that time, the man had a different name. The dog wasn't the same, either. Instead of asking for the money outright, he gave her the link for the animal hospital, so she could send the money to them as opposed to giving it to him."

Her mother held up her wine glass as she spoke. "That sounds legit."

"On the surface, maybe," Nala agreed. "Turns out the animal hospital is an actual one, but they didn't have the account."

Her father grunted around a mouthful of food, then swallowed and added, "The best cons are those with actual business or real people names. People are reassured, hearing the names, although few bother checking to see if they're legit."

"I checked." There was some rustling in the kitchen that concerned her. A quick cut of her eyes to her mother showed either her mother didn't hear it or wasn't concerned. She found the last unbelievable. She continued on with her answer. "The animal hospital has been around a long time. However, they don't accept online payments. What would be the point since you have to bring in your animal?"

"Someone is using the animal hospital name to gain funds. That's fraud and larceny, since he's stealing from these women. We need to find out who created that pay link."

A crash sounded in the kitchen, causing the three of them to snap their heads toward the door. Max shot through the door with a ham bone in his mouth. He ran toward the front door, then switched directions since it was closed and surged up the stairs.

Her mother glanced in the direction the shepherd had fled. Instead of being mad, she merely shook her head. "I should have guessed leaving the bone in the kitchen trash was a mistake."

Nala was already up and in pursuit of her dog, but paused at the stairs. "I'm sorry. He's usually not like this." *What a lie.* Still, he was usually on his good behavior at her parents' house. "He's a rescue dog and spent some time on the streets. I guess sometimes he reverts."

She hustled up the stairs, anxious to get the bone away from Max before he rubbed the greasy thing all over her mother's oriental carpets. Sometimes, her dog could be a jerk.

AFTER THE KITCHEN disaster, Nala expected to grab her dog and leave, but her parents wouldn't hear of it. Instead, her mother grabbed Max by the collar and led him to the mudroom to think about his actions. Instead of howling at being locked in a room with the overpowering scent of fabric softener sheets, he accepted his punishment or possibly fell asleep with a full stomach.

Over pie and coffee, they discussed her latest case that Karly had dubbed Dog Park Romeo. She enjoyed the sweet tang of the cherry pie as her father spoke.

"Surely you can get Elvin to follow up on the link. I know I could probably do likewise at the station, but no one has sworn out a complaint against your Dog Park Romeo, yet." He waggled his eyebrows. "Elvin has some unorthodox methods, but they're effective. Good chance we would be stonewalled by the company, stating privacy laws and all that."

She wrinkled her nose. She'd heard this tirade before. "Dad, you wouldn't want them giving out your information to anyone who asks."

"Maybe not," he grudgingly agreed, "but we're the police. We need that information."

"I'm sure you'd get it if you had a warrant."

"Probably, but by that time, it would be too late. That's why Elvin is a much better option." He held up his hand as if stopping traffic. "Don't tell me his methods. I'm better off not knowing."

"Good, because I don't know." Nala mused as she picked up her coffee cup.

Her nerdy high school friend served as a consultant and was able to do some high-level computer hacking and did security consulting for several notable agencies. If Elvin couldn't get something done, he knew someone who could.

"I take it you've had no luck tracking the man down."

Her attempt at undercover work ended in a fiasco that made her sigh heavily. "I tried with Karly, but she brought some super out-of-control dog that had everyone clearing out in a hurry."

"That's odd." Her mother wrinkled her nose as if something smelled wrong to her. "She has countless dogs she could have used. Why not use a nice, well-behaved poodle?"

Sometimes her mother, for all her celebrated business acumen, missed out on the obvious. "I'm betting they don't get that many perfect, well-behaved purebred dogs in the shelter. It happens now and then, but breed rescue associations sweep in and take the dogs.

It's more likely they get half-grown puppies or bored dogs who destroy homes. They recently had an adoption promotion where you could adopt any animal for only five dollars. It cleared out their kennels. This dog just came in, and it's obvious why it was surrendered. Apparently, the owners couldn't control it."

"Not a good choice if Karly was trying to get a man to talk to her." Her mother stated the obvious.

A giggle escaped as Nala recalled her best friend's awkward gait in her stiletto boots while being pulled by the large dog. "It was rather funny. Worse, she had fixed herself up as if heading off to speed dating. I'm not sure that's the type of woman our Dog Park Romeo goes for."

"Ha!" Her father slapped the table. "I'd think not. There should have been plenty of single men there that would have tried to make her acquaintance."

"On a normal day, there'd be one or two guys who might try to talk to her, but she had this huge, out-of-control dog running full tilt toward the park. People were grabbing their dogs and fleeing. It was probably the fastest the park has ever emptied."

Her father continued to chuckle, even to the point of wiping his eyes with the back of his hand. "Do you think anyone videotaped it and put it online?"

While many awkward moments, along with a few life-threatening ones, were filmed by those gawking nearby, she hadn't witnessed anyone who stayed long enough to film Karly's race across the park. "I don't think so."

If they had and did post it, it would ruin using Karly as a decoy. Nala shook her head slowly. "I certainly hope not. It's a shame she couldn't have used a better-behaved dog. Still, it's good that the shelter manages to place so many dogs."

"Why not use Max?" her father suggested. "He's well-trained. I work with him every time you two come over."

He did and to refuse to use the dog he specifically trained would be an insult to her father. Still, Max could be a wild card. Most books on dog training insisted that the dog wanted to please you. She was fairly sure Max wanted to please himself first. A silence stretched out, almost reaching the awkward point, when her mother intervened.

"I don't think the dog is the problem. However, I would have to admit an out-of-control dog would make it hard to hold a conversation. I think it might be the woman." She gestured to Nala. "You young women don't realize how good you have it with your firm bodies and unwrinkled skin. Instead, you spend your time rejecting decent men for trivial reasons."

"Mom, is that relevant?" It sounded more like she was warming up for her rant about wanting grandchildren. However, it did keep Nala from answering her father's inquiry about Max.

"It is." She reached for her napkin and dabbed at her lips. As Graham pushed back his chair and stood, she added, "Hear me out,"

"I will as soon as I let Max out," Graham promised. "I think he has spent enough time in the laundry room for doing what dogs do. They're scavengers. If Gwen hadn't placed the ham bone in such a tempting location, Max wouldn't have fallen prey to his basic instincts."

Her mother, who always believed in excellent posture, somehow straightened her back even more, giving it a ramrod appearance. "It's *my* fault?"

The tone of her voice signaled she was more than a little miffed. It was time to go.

Nala made a point of looking at her watch. "Look at that! It's almost three, and I promised Elvin I would meet him to go over the cases." She jumped up and shot her mother an apologetic smile. "Sorry, I can't help with the dishes, but work calls. I'll grab my dog and go."

Gwen managed a dramatic sigh and glared at her husband. "See? You made our only child scurry away."

"Me?"

She could hear her father through the kitchen door as she headed to the laundry room to free Max. The coward's way would be to leave through the back door, but if she did, she'd never hear the end of it.

Max backed up as she opened the door and managed to act chastened over his earlier misdeed. Most people would have bought it, but because she knew her dog so well, she didn't. "Never mind the apologetic dog act. I know better. We need to get out of here as quickly as possible."

The snap of the leash echoed against the wall of appliances. Normally, she would have put it on at the door, but why take any chances after the day she'd just had? As they entered the dining room, she noticed her parents were no longer trading barbs and were having a light-hearted conversation. Did anyone ever understand their parents?

Her mother pointed a dessert fork at Nala. "I never finished what I was saying. I'm not sure how old your clients are, but I assume they're much older than you."

While Nala never made it a practice to ask for her client's age, her observation skills were reasonably sharp. "They are. Probably twenty years or so."

Her mother grinned, then shot a triumphant look at her husband. "Exactly as I thought. A woman that age doesn't expect casual conversation from a good-looking man. She probably wouldn't even expect it to be of a romantic nature and would possibly prolong it."

Her mother was right about the age. She hated when her mother made a valid observation before she did. Gwen Bonne always had to be the best at everything, which left precious little for Nala to excel at. Sleuthing was her thing.

"They both stated they went on a date with the man."

"Was it a date?" her mother asked with one arched eyebrow.

She assumed it was, because the women said so. "I guess it all depends on what they consider a date."

Max pulled at his lead and whimpered. Sure, he was playing a part or at least she thought he was. "I gotta go." She angled her head in Max's direction. "He does, too."

Goodbyes were exchanged as Nala shouldered on her jacket before opening the door. Once outside, Max made an extended survey of the yard, sniffing at every winter brown shrub and tree.

In the car, she asked, "Was that walk really necessary?"

"They were looking out the windows."

She blew out a breath. She should have suspected as much. The car engine turned over as she contemplated actually visiting Elvin as she had implied. With any luck, he might come up with some high-tech ways to catch her dog-lover whisperer.

"I think it might be beneficial to see Elvin."

"Bark! Bark! He has the best dog treats."

In truth, Elvin didn't have any dog treats. He simply gave Max the same beef jerky he enjoyed and bought for himself.

Chapter Five

THERE WERE WIRES, tools, and assorted electronic bits that Nala didn't recognize scattered across Elvin's table. He was always in the middle of building some high-tech prototype that would make him a millionaire. It hadn't happened yet, which was why he took her piddly cases.

"What can you do for me as far as helping me catch this callous heartbreaker?"

"Heartbreaker, huh?" Elvin stroked the stubble on his chin as he pondered the situation. "From what you told me, your clients only went out on one date. There seems to be a vagueness of what the date consisted of. I hardly see how that makes the man a heartbreaker."

"Come on." She growled the words. "Quit thinking like a man. As soon as the suspect strolled over to talk to the women, they were spinning scenarios in their mind of walking side by side on the park path with their dogs."

He attempted his best De Niro imitation. "You talking to me?"

"Enough of the movie quotes. I'm on a tight timetable here. Even though I'm not working at the school anymore, I did promise to help the new teacher by catching up with where the class should be."

"Your funeral, pal."

He held up his hand, knowing what she would say. "I'll stop. As for the women thinking there would be a happy-ever-after, that's their problem. Maybe the guy was just bored and wanted to talk to someone."

Max placed his head on the table and moved enough to send the electronic bits tumbling.

Elvin shoved to his feet. "Okay, okay, I'll get you some jerky. Nala, Max is an extortion artist." He pointed to Max, who had backed away from the table and was avidly tracking Elvin.

"Tell me about it. At least he didn't make you think of long runs together and rolling over in the grass with your feet kicking up in the air."

"True. I did think he'd be a better wingman than he was. Chicks dig dogs. The only problem was the chick's boyfriend wasn't all that fond of *me*."

Even though it may have bothered Elvin, she couldn't stop herself from laughing. "I got some excellent undercover props out of it."

He located the plastic container of jerky and tossed a strip to Max who caught it in mid-air, then carried it to the table. A little treat now and then Max could handle, but not an entire container of jerky. It would shoot his sodium level sky high.

"Don't even think of feeding my dog all that jerky," she warned.

"I'm not." Elvin kept his arms wrapped protectively around the plastic container as he sat. "You saw Max watch me. He knew where the container was and might decide to help himself. Bison jerky is not cheap."

"That's why Max has to come here to get any." She winked at her friend. Her canine did have a little help-himself attitude. As her Dad would say, it was just dogs being dogs. Right up there with boys being boys. Still, it always seemed like when she did something that was girls just being girls, she'd gotten grounded.

"Let's get back to the case. Even my father remarked on the women not being on a real date. Why would this matter? Especially when he solicited money under a false pretense to help his sick dog?"

"Technically, it shouldn't." He gave up his death grip on the jerky and placed it on the table. "Let's say the female in question is you. You're hanging out at the park with Max with no real plans to meet anyone when an attractive stranger comes up and starts talking to you. What is your first thought?"

"Ack!" She stuck out her tongue. "Don't talk to me. My hair is a mess, and I forgot to brush my teeth before I left. Worse, I have on my oldest sweats."

Elvin leaned back in his chair and audibly exhaled. "Alrighty then, let's pretend you're not so vain and did brush your teeth before coming to the park."

She gave a derisive snort. "I'm not vain. If I were vain, I'd toss my hair back and glance up at the man through half-closed eyes. Of course, he *is* coming over to talk to me. The teeth, the hair, the clothes are normal thoughts. Any woman might have them."

His fingers drummed on the table top. "Did you ask them what they were wearing?"

"No, I didn't."

"You should, especially if you're doing undercover work to entice your hustler into an investigative web. If you need to know his green light, then you could be it."

He had a valid point. It didn't happen all the time, but when it did, he nailed it. "You're right. My mother suggested that the women weren't all that young and would welcome the attention of a younger, attractive male."

He whistled, wiggled his eyebrows, and said, "Boy toy."

"Get your mind out of the gutter. The ladies who came to my office were quiet, conservative sorts. Not the type to flaunt a younger boyfriend."

"Sounds to me like you have your type."

"True enough. Neither of them showed up in revealing clothing. Although in this frigid weather, I'd be hard-pressed to imagine anyone at the dog park with cleavage-baring tops."

"You'd be surprised." He laced his fingers behind his head and kicked back the chair to balance on two legs.

"You? Dog park? You don't even own a dog."

He lowered his chair. "That was a sticking point. I claimed my dog had died, and I had returned for sentimental reasons."

She shot him a skeptical look and snorted.

He held out his hands, palms up. "It's hard meeting single women. The dog park didn't work out that well without a dog. That's why your scammer has a dog."

"My clients complained about a man named Edward and another one named Allan. Madeline said he resembled a young Mark Harmon from NCIS."

"He has gray hair?"

"She did say *young*."

"Okay. At least you have a visual. However, sometimes it's difficult with women when it comes to descriptions. They're always jazzing things up to make things sound better."

That Elvin never held back on his beliefs or stereotypes as most men did was no secret. It didn't mean the other men didn't have similar thoughts. They were just smart enough not to voice them. The man was lucky he now had a girlfriend who could see past his macho façade.

She held both hands up and made an hourglass shape and lowered her voice to emulate a male. "Whoa, man, you should have seen her. She had measurements that could bring a dead man back to life." She licked her finger and made a sizzling sound.

"I'm not that bad!"

"You were before Amy. The woman has had a positive effect on you. Anyhow, I can agree that women might make things sound better for their girlfriends or even family members. I'm a private investigator. If they want me to find the dude, they've got to shoot straight with me."

"I agree. Still, why didn't they go to the police?"

It had been her first question. "Mostly, they had no clue a crime had been committed. They just thought they'd made a stupid mistake. Lois said she wanted something bad to happen to the man, preferably something permanent. What she really wanted was to alert other women he was out there, without her name entering into it. It's a tricky situation. If I want to catch the guy or guys, and I do, I can't run around telling everyone about the Dog Park Romeo. It would scare the guy away. He might even move on to another city."

"Okay." Elvin held up one finger, ignoring Max who was doing his best to push past the arm barrier to the bison treats. "Client number one wants women to be forewarned. What does your second client want?"

"Her money back." She gave a little nod as if the question was a no-brainer. "She'd also prefer something horrible to happen to Edward, such as being doused in honey and tied to a fire ant mound."

"Sounds angry."

"Just a tad. She really didn't have the money to lose."

"What do you want from me?"

"I want to catch the slime bag or bags, since I'm not sure if it's one guy or a pair, or even random men trying the same con. I wish I could get more info without blowing my cover. Both women could give us a little more of the puzzle. Successful liars always use a little bit of the truth. If they made everything up, there would be no way they could remember it. His middle name might be Allan or Edward, but no one knows it or calls him by that name."

"Kinda like dating profiles."

"Exactly. What can you do for me as far as gadgets?"

Elvin pushed Max away. "Call off your dog, first."

She whistled. Max gave a canine sigh, walked over to where she sat, and flopped on the floor. "The man or men are guilty of fraud, wire fraud for using online payment, and larceny. The wire fraud makes them guilty of the RICO law, also. Tack on to it getting a woman's hopes up who has long given up on romance. I think that may be the worst."

Elvin held up his hands about a foot apart. "Here's what I can do. I can make a special collar for Max. It would have a listening device and a tiny camera. The downside is you would see the man from the knees down. Never great for identification. We need our decoy to wear a camera, too."

"That's doable. The only problem is anything we record without the scammer's permission is not admissible in court."

"That's all I got for you. It could be enough for the police to bring him in if you're willing to try."

"You bet I am." Max surged to his feet and barked twice. "He's in, too," Nala added, just in case her canine decided to talk. Even though she had told him several times nothing good would come of speaking in front of others, there were still accidents. She tried to cover them up by coughing or clearing her throat. A few times she'd claimed it was her and her awful allergies.

"Let me measure Max's neck, and I'll get to work on it. It might be better to be a tag of sorts. At least that would hang free of his huge ruff of hair. It would be a shame if all we got was close-ups of his neck hair."

Before Max could grumble, Nala gave him a warning pat on the head. "It might be better just to concentrate on the transmitter. A camera probably wouldn't work."

"Wait." Elvin stood, strolled out of the room, then came back with a metal tape measure. "This is all I could find. It should give us a general idea." He knelt and wrapped the ribbon of metal around Max's neck. The metal flexed and pinged, causing Max to twitch his ears. "Almost done."

Elvin stood, grabbed a sheet of paper on the table, pulled a pen from his pocket, and wrote down a number. "Got it. Anything else?"

"Not really." Nala stood. "I appreciate it. Give me a call when it's done." She slapped her leg as an indication for Max to follow. He surged to his feet with his tail making a slow wag as they both approached the door. At the exit, Nala turned slightly and called back over her shoulder. "How did you know Amy was the one?"

Her friend shrugged. "She liked me for who I am."

Good answer.

Chapter Six

THE KEYS RATTLED as Nala tossed them into a wooden bowl by the front door. Her father pointed out on more than one occasion that it made them ideal for an opportunist thief. Quite frankly, if she tried to be too clever with where she put things, she'd never get out of the house. The phone usually rested beside the wooden bowl, hooked up to its charger. She hesitated at plugging in the phone.

While driving, it had gone off several times. She'd ignored it, not even bothering to pick it up to see who was calling. One chime, she recognized as Karly, who would want to rehash the undercover fiasco. The other was the Death March from a popular science fiction movie she used for her mother. Fortunately, her mother was unfamiliar with the movie. No need to listen to her endless helpful clues on how to be a better businesswoman. A few noteworthy ones came with other advice she'd rather not hear. Then, there was a third call, an unknown number. It might be important.

Max jostled her arm and announced, "I'm hungry."

"Not sure how you can be. Today has been an endless feast for you." She strolled into the kitchen and picked up his dish. Even though she bought the organic kibble that listed chicken as its first ingredient, he could be picky. She shook some food into his bowl and mused about who could have called her. It could have been Tyler. Instead of putting the bowl down for him, she walked back to the living room to get her phone.

Max complained from the kitchen. "What's the deal? Do you expect me to knock it down from the counter? Last time, you yelled when I did that!"

"I will again! Just wait a second." She lunged back into the kitchen with her phone in one hand and put the dog food on the floor. "There."

Max went over to the dish, sniffed it, and glanced up. "Is that it?"

"It is. This isn't a doggy diner."

"I should say not. On second thought, I want to go outside and eat some grass."

The suggestion made her groan, knowing the inevitable results of grass eating. She opened the door, realizing it was probably what her dog needed. She stood just inside the sliding glass doors and put her voice mail on speaker. That was the great thing about living alone: no one complaining about her listening to her voicemail on speaker. There was also eating cereal for supper. That was the extent of the list. With Max, she couldn't really even say she was living alone. If she wanted to talk to someone, she had Max. His advice was a little odd. He told her she always had the option of chasing the neighbor's cat to lift her mood.

The first voice mail was from Karly, wanting her to know that the former owners of the out-of-control dog that her friend brought to the park came back for him, which surely should be classified as a miracle. The second was her mother, who offered to do undercover work for her since she knew how it was done. That either meant she'd watched a crime drama or heard her father talk. She would discourage her mother by telling her she was too glamorous for the job, an excuse she'd readily accept.

The third caller identified herself. "Hello? This is Deidre. Tyler, I mean Officer Goodnight, gave me your number. Things feel off with my current squeeze."

A significant pause in the message prompted Nala to retort, "Drop the man."

"It's just that I love him, but..."

Another long pause had Nala wondering if the woman had hung up before her voice sounded again.

"As a police officer, especially one involved in narcotics, I can't take chances. He checks out clean, but something feels wrong. I called your office, and there was no answer. Didn't think you worked on Sundays, but I was hoping. Call me back." She ended by stating her number.

The woman sounded as if she was on the verge of tears. Each pause was probably her choking back a sob. Like most women who came to her to check out their sweetheart or husband, she already knew something was wrong. She probably denied it for a while, too, not wanting to give up on her man. He must have some redeeming qualities if she was willing to shuck out the money for an information search.

As an officer of the law, the woman could search for arrests, traffic tickets, even his credit score. Whether she liked it or not, Nala was probably the woman's last hope, aside from asking the man if something was up. It only worked if he wasn't trying to hide anything, in which case the woman wouldn't need to ask.

She pressed in the numbers as she wondered if Tyler had been involved with the luscious Deidre. She hadn't sounded particularly luscious, just upset. Most women would offload a suspicious acting guy in a hurry, especially if they hadn't been dating long. That would mean Deidre had been dating the sneaky guy for a while, which would mean she hadn't been dating Tyler. She exhaled heavily and opened the door for Max.

Still concentrating on the matter, she hadn't completed the phone number and received an error message for her trouble. "Snickerdoodles!" She shook her head and tried the number again while talking to herself. "Tyler can date anyone he wants."

"Hello?" A voice said at the other end. "I agree. Tyler can date anyone he wants. What Tyler are we talking about?"

She closed her eyes. *Really*? She just did that. "Sorry. I was talking to someone else. I shouldn't have been doing that while the phone was ringing."

"No problem. Is this Nala? The private eye?"

"It is." However, it would have been hard to tell by how she answered the phone. "Nala Bonne, I was responding to your message."

"Thank you. I know I need to come into your office and sign a contract or something."

"True. If you can give me your boyfriend's name, maybe social, anything else you think might be helpful, I can do some preliminary checking. I can let you know what I find before I go any further."

"Would you? That's more than I expected on a weekend."

"You're in luck. I don't have any big plans."

"Good." Deidre cleared her throat. "I mean not good that you don't have plans, but good you can start right away."

"I know what you meant. Let me get some paper and a pen so I can write this down." She suited her actions to her words. She managed to find a receipt with a blank back and a thick tip permanent marker. "Go ahead."

"His name is Magnus Lee McGee."

"His parents must not have liked him much."

"I said something similar to him when I met him."

"Where did you meet?"

"At The Blue Line, a cop bar at—"

"I know where it is."

"Yeah, I guess you would with your, ah, father and all."

Of course, she knew her father. Everyone did. "No worries. This will not be mentioned to my father. I major in being discreet."

"Good to know. He's a broker, deals mainly in international funds. He comes from old money, too. Here's his social." She rattled off his number and had Nala repeat it back, before continuing. "I'm in my car in my driveway. It was fortunate you called as I was just arriving home. Can't stay on the phone too long or Magnus could look out and wonder who I'm talking to."

"Magnus lives with you?"

"He has for the past six months."

A red flag popped up in her mind and waved wildly. "Let's set a time tomorrow."

"Could you make it early? I have to work. I can go in a little late and say I had a dentist appointment. Still, I'll have to call ahead to alert everyone at work about the appointment."

"How about eight?"

Max whimpered.

"Eight, it is. I know where the office is. Officer Goodnight pointed it out to me."

"Good to know." It would be better to know on what occasion he'd point it out. Did he add anything when he did so, such as there's this crazy chick I tried to date once or equally unflattering remarks? To be fair, he was the one who had a pregnant old girlfriend show up on the scene, insisting he'd help her. His defense was she was a friend, not a girlfriend.

"See you then."

"Looking forward to it."

She hung up the phone and waited a few seconds before calling Elvin. He picked up on the first ring. "Whadya got for me?"

"Magnus Lee McGee, full search, even the dark stuff. Got a call from a worried girlfriend."

"Is he missing?"

"Not in the physical sense. Something isn't right about him."

"You mean besides having a name like a cartoon character?"

"You're thinking of Mr. Magoo, and I doubt his first name was Magnus. Call me back when you find something."

A grumble carried over the phone. "You're assuming this guy is dirty."

"Call it woman's intuition. I'll be doing my part from this end by combing social media and the newspapers."

"Yeah, yeah, you need to remember that just because you don't have a social life doesn't necessarily imply other people don't. You're in luck, though. I can put in the search parameters, then go pick up Amy. By the time I come back, the search should be finished."

It would be nice if he got back to her tonight, but there was nothing she could do about it if he didn't. Elvin was the best there was in obtaining information. She'd wait. "Sounds good," she said, when she really meant, I'll have to wait until you get back to me.

She hung up and turned her attention to Max. Stretched out on the couch, hogging it from end to end, and seeing she was off the phone, he spoke in a cajoling tone. "It sure would be nice if someone turned on the television to the classic movie channel. There's a *Rin Tin Tin* marathon."

Instead of asking how he knew, she turned on the television and headed off to get her computer. After about twenty minutes, she discovered Magnus had no social media accounts. With a name like that, he sounded like he had some age on him. Maybe the Internet didn't appeal.

Another ten minutes proved he never made the newspapers. Deidre said something about old money. Nothing she could find. Some of the McGees migrated from Scotland in the 19th century. There was a minister named McGee who clogged the pages of her search. She doubted that was the source of Magnus's money, although some of those televangelists were as rich as Midas. If Magnus came from old money and was a successful stockbroker, why would he move in with a cop? A cop didn't make the bucks. Depending on when Deidre started working, she should be making a salary in the forties, possibly fifties. Her house would be a modest one, not exactly a reason a man would leave behind the family estate or an inground pool. It would be more reasonable for him to invite *her* to live with him. Then again, he could be lying about being from old money.

Chapter Seven

D UE TO IT being winter, it was still dark when she shoved Max out of the house. He turned and tried to dash back through the door. "It's still night. You've lost your mind."

"It's a little after seven, and we're going to have to book it to get to the office before Deidre does. Thank goodness Sawyer shows up early. Even if she gets there before us, he can get her a cup of coffee and turn on that Minnesota nice of his. No woman would mind having to spend time enjoying his wholesome good looks. That man should be a model for the L. L. Bean Catalog."

"You don't spend much time in the office appreciating the Minnesota vice."

"It's *nice*, not *vice*. Get in the car." She swung open the passenger door and waited for her dog to settle in before walking to the driver side. As for Max's comments, she'd made sure not to like Sawyer too much. She needed his portion of the rent. There could be no romantic relationship between them, possibly ending with one getting mad and moving away. Besides, she thought of him as a cousin, a very attractive cousin.

The roads were already packed with shift workers and obviously more than a few of them were late, indicated by their driving. Fortunately, she knew a few shortcuts that involved back roads, plus cutting through a neighborhood and a mall parking lot to avoid congestion. To avoid a wreck, she drove up on the shoulder to pass, which was a major traffic no-no, but others followed her bold action.

Her usual parking spot was taken by a red compact, which may have been Deidre's car. She had to park in front of Sawyer's pickup, which meant a little longer walk. "We're here. Let's hit it."

Max chose to pick his way across the console as opposed to leaping out of the car as he usually did. "Hit what? I didn't feel anything."

"It's an expression. It means hurry, which you should do now. Walk close to me. I don't have time for a leash."

"Then you *must* be in a hurry." Max's paws hit the pavement and chose to do a full circle of the car, sniffing the curb, the street, and the sidewalk.

"Come on, it's where we always park. It smells the same."

"No. We usually park eight feet farther down. It smells different here. Hey, look. I found a fast food wrapper." He poked his nose at a yellow wrapper.

"I'm getting the leash."

His head came up abruptly. "Someone got up on the wrong side of the bed." He left the paper and trotted to Nala's side. "I'm ready to *hit* it."

Thankfully, there were no more incidents, even when a woman leading a poodle on a sparkly chain strolled by. She managed to get Max inside the building with no problems. Once she got upstairs, she'd give him a treat. "I'm really proud of how you ignored that poodle."

"Please. Fifi strolls by the building every day trying to get my attention."

"Uh-huh." No need to mention Fifi's owner lived in one of the apartments in the building. "Remember, no talking."

"Bark! Bark!"

"Keep it that way." She pasted on a professional smile as she jogged up the steps. Her plan to get a special investigator's wardrobe composed of black, navy, and khaki to blend in hadn't worked out as well as she'd hoped. The lack of excess money had her using her preschool teacher outfits, substituting a plain tee for anything glittery or that had embroidered crayons or school buses on it.

The soft rumble of Sawyer's baritone meant he was keeping Deidre entertained. The man deserved a treat, but something a little better than the dog biscuit Max was going to get. A coffee card or she could buy him lunch. The door wasn't even latched. A push opened it, and Max rushed in as usual. A yelp had to have come from Deidre. Sawyer was used to Max.

"No worries," Sawyer reassured an attractive woman who clutched a coffee cup while giving Max a dubious stare.

"He's mine," Nala stated the obvious as she walked in. "Nala Bonne." She held out her hand.

The woman switched the coffee cup to her left hand to shake. "Deidre Williams."

"Thanks for waiting. I had good intentions of being here before you." She shrugged. "Traffic." She gestured to the interior office, the door held open by the hopelessly tacky dog statue she'd unearthed in the basement. Because her mother ran an interior design firm, she enjoyed using objects now and then that horrified her. Besides, it was so ugly, it was endearing.

Deidre strolled by and took the client chair. Before Nala could remove the statue and shut the door, Max rushed in and caught her eye as he laid beside the desk. She would have sworn he winked. There was no way she'd get Max to leave. Her best bet was to make it look intentional.

"This is Max, my investigative partner. He's excellent at tailing folks and knows when someone is lying."

"How does he do that?"

"It must be the scent a person puts out. He barks when they're lying." She had no clue how he did it, but it made sense to her. After all, lie detectors depended on increased heart rate and sweaty palms. Why not dogs?

Deidre leaned forward to give Max another look. "That would be helpful. Is it hard to get him into places so he can give everyone a good sniff?"

"My best bet is going someplace where people are already outside. Then I can just be walking my specially trained dog."

"Very cool." Deidre pulled out her smartphone and glanced at it. "I really need to hurry. I got someone covering for me, but she has her own workload to handle. Show me the contract. I'll pay and be on my way."

Nala had several types of pre-made contracts made out. It always gave her a little thrill when she could use one. It made her feel like a real gumshoe. The fictional PIs like Sam Spade or Phillip Marlowe did business with a handshake, not a contract. In her short time as an investigator, she'd had a contract save her from a tight place when demanding customers wanted more service than they'd paid for.

She pulled out the short information sweep, which she nicknamed *Don't Date a Liar.* "Here you go." She centered the paper in front of Deidre. "This covers if he is using his real name. Does he work where he said he does? Did he really graduate from Harvard or any school? Is he married? Is he in debt? Is he a player?"

"How can you tell if a man is a player?"

"It's fairly easy on social media. Sometimes, I can do it by just matching his photo to several accounts where he uses different names. If he goes by a single name, preferably his own, I look him up on the dating rating apps."

"They have that?" Deidre questioned.

"Yep. Some folks are ruthless on it. One even lets people such as your family or friends talk you up. Anyone can jump on and check it out. Before you go out with a guy you can see what someone else says."

Deidre reached for a pen, but instead of signing the contract, she pointed the writing implement at Nala. "You find anything out last night?"

"No social media. None."

"Yeah, I know. Weird, huh? It's like he's ninety instead of forty. He's not even cool with me posting a picture of us on my site."

The old don't-show-my-picture-around-baby usually spelled *married.* Still, if Magnus lived with Deidre for the past six months, it would be hard to run that past any wife. "Didn't that make you suspicious?"

"It did. That's when I ran a background check on him. No criminal history. Not married. Good credit."

"Looks like you did my job for me." She held up her hands ready to say goodbye to an easy hundred and fifty.

"No." She shook her head. "Something isn't right, and I'm not imagining it. That's what Magnus always tells me when I ask. Sometimes, I swear the man is gaslighting me. You know, like in that old movie where the man kept moving stuff around to make his wife doubt her own sanity. That's been happening."

Elvin would know the movie. She'd ask him later when he called. "Like what?"

"My purse wasn't where I left it. My phone was turned off when I know it was on. I got into my car after I filled up just the other day and only have half a tank. Magnus swears he has no clue what I'm talking about."

"Could you have put your purse somewhere else?"

"Yes," Deidre admitted but didn't sound convinced of the fact. "I might have turned my phone off, too. There was no way I misplaced a half tank of gas, though." Deidre continued. "Just look into this for me. Use your investigative dog, too." She picked up the pen and signed the contract.

Nala watched the woman write and had a mental image of money flying into her account. Still, she needed to ask her the hard question. She steepled her fingers together and arranged her face into a somber expression. "If I do come up with some uncomfortable information, are you at a place where you're willing to listen?"

"I'm here, aren't I?"

"Most women come to me when they assume their significant other is cheating. I discovered one of the husbands was embezzling from his company. The wife didn't want me to report him since he wasn't stepping out on her."

Deidre scooted forward in her chair. "You reported him, right?"

"You bet I did. A crime is still a crime even if your wife doesn't care. So, I'm asking…"

"I want to know everything. I'm a big girl. I can handle it." She took out her wallet and pulled out a gold card. "I noticed the sign on your door says you take credit cards."

"Let me get the square reader up. Believe it or not," she grinned at her newest client, "you're my first customer of the day. She put the jack into the phone and tapped the app to ready it. The card went in easy. All she had to do was wait to make sure it went through. The signature window popped up. "Okay. Sign here. I can send a receipt to your email."

"No receipt." Deidre shook her head emphatically. "I don't want Magnus to know I've been here."

"Do you think he's reading your email and checking your phone?"

She tucked her card back into her wallet as she spoke. "Let's put it this way, I'm not sure if he doesn't. It's better to be safe."

"Okay." It served as her go-to word when she didn't know what else to say. Personally, if Deidre was a friend, she'd tell her to leave now, then contact a lawyer to remove Magnus from the premise. "Before you go, how long ago did you run the background check?"

"Six months."

"Okay." There was that word again. After the check, which must have been routine for someone working in narcotics, she invited Magnus to live with her, after ascertaining the man had no criminal history.

Deidre stood up to leave, which caused Nala to grab the contract. "Wait. Let me make you a copy of the contract."

She waved her hand, causing her car keys to rattle. "No copies. No papers. It might be better if I called you or you can call me at my work number to set up a meet." She pulled a card out of an inside pocket and handed it to Nala, then left.

Weird. Her gut told her there was a great deal going on with Magnus. It sounded more like Deidre was doing deep cover work as opposed to living with a man she supposedly loved. Well, that jump-started her day. The scent of coffee had her returning to the outer office. As she poured herself a cup, Sawyer came out from behind his desk and sat on the edge of it.

"Do you remember me telling you about my best friend?"

"Yeah." Actually, she didn't. It must have been one of those conversations she had blocked out. Sawyer was a chatty dude. It was one of the reasons she did most of her work on the road, at home, or in a nearby coffee shop. "It was Robert? Michael?"

"Damien. Surely you would have remembered that name. At school, we used to tease him because of that old movie with the kid named Damien who was the antichrist or something. We used to call him Demon Seed."

"There's a unique nickname." She enjoyed a sip of the robust coffee.

"Good old Demon Seed. Anyhow, Damien is all busted up about his divorce. I was trying to think of a way to cheer him up. I told him he could do whatever he wanted now. His soon-to-be ex *was* a bit controlling."

"I guess he's going to buy a sports car now."

"Oh, no. He already has one. Cherry red." Sawyer grinned. "He's going to sell it to me since it isn't part of the settlement. All Damien wants to do now is to take a tour around the world."

"That would take some time. At least eighty days if he uses a hot air balloon." Nala laughed at her joke but realized Sawyer didn't get it. "It's a book and movie. *Around the World in Eighty Days?*"

"I don't think it will take that long. He just wants to hit the prime spots."

"Which are?" She might want to know if she ever saved up enough money to travel abroad.

"Oh, you know, anywhere there's hot women with an accent." His grin grew wider as he continued. "On the lookout for two swinging Minnesotan guys."

"Okay, stop." She held up her hand. "This is a joke, right? No one uses swinging and Minnesotan together. Is this all some enormous gag?"

The smile slipped from Sawyer's face. "Do you think I would lie to you? I know we haven't been working together long. I came here because I wanted a fresh start. Now, Damien needs a fresh start, and I need to be there for him."

"When are you leaving?" Bye-bye extra rent money and all-around Boy Friday, too. She rather liked having someone in the office when a possible client came by when she was out.

"It depends when the divorce is finalized. It could be this week. I'll let you know the night before."

Technically, he didn't work for her. They only shared an office, which meant two weeks' notice wasn't necessary. At least he'd paid this month's rent. With Sawyer gone, she couldn't get by on looking up bad boyfriends of hustlers in the dog park. She'd need a steady income stream.

Why now? Especially after she finally gave up subbing at her old preschool job. She couldn't get it back. The position was filled. She should know since she'd trained her replacement.

"Aren't you excited about my trip around the world?"

Nala took a long sip from her coffee cup, not tasting it as the possibility of losing her business rammed into the image of her mother saying *I told you so*. What was she going to do? Sawyer was staring at her. He expected a happy response.

"Yay for you. What a lucky guy you are. You get to go on an endless trip with your embittered friend trying to chat up women who don't speak English and are only interested in your money."

Sawyer sighed, then walked back around his desk. "Harry told me you were bad at pep talks."

Yeah, I am.

Her phone chimed with a message from Elvin: *Need to talk to you.*

Chapter Eight

THE RADIO IN Nala's car was playing a catchy tune. The music lifted her mood somewhat. She drummed her hand on the steering wheel to the beat while she waited for the light to change. She was on her way to Elvin's place. Wouldn't most subcontractors come to her? Her lips pursed as she considered the possibility. Elvin was her only sub-contractor and was good at what he did. He probably took the place of two or three subcontractors. If he wanted to lay low in his residence that was his business. However, he'd always meet her for lunch if she were paying.

The shock of Sawyer leaving so abruptly was wearing off a little. It is what it is. Life was all about changes, which meant she had no choice but to roll with them. Another upbeat song came on—Nala caught herself singing along until Max started howling.

Nala switched the station, causing Max to shoot her an annoyed look.

"That was just mean."

"Please," Nala sighed, knowing she'd hear the repeat of the same argument she'd heard before. "I do realize you were singing,"

"So were you."

"It's a small car. Too small to hold your majestic howl." She learned early on that her rescue pooch was a tad oversensitive.

"You got that right. At least I had the words right."

No reason to reply, she reminded herself. True, she occasionally did make up words when she couldn't remember the lyrics. It took skill to come up with words fast that fit and made sense. Ordinary people settled for singing the actual words. Instead, she drove without saying a word. The all-news station she had tuned to chattered on about weather, then moved on to traffic.

It took another twenty minutes to reach Elvin's house without a word being exchanged. The sign for the neighborhood would never let people know a hacking mastermind resided within. Elvin confided once that he worked hard to ensure his yard and home would not attract too much attention. A showy place would attract some envy and a lot of attention while an overgrown yard would merit grumbling. Elvin hired a yard service to take care of his lawn, which surprised Nala that he'd let anyone get that close.

Before she even pulled into the driveway, the security system already had tracked her car and notified Elvin someone was coming along with a visual image. He had so many security devices installed it made her wonder if the neighbors treated that as unusual.

She bumped into the driveway and the garage door opened. Weird. It meant Elvin wanted her to pull in next to his sports car he had once labeled as *The Babe Mobile*. His recent girlfriend labeled the car with another word—*compensation*. It made Nala wonder if there was a new car in his future.

Nala stayed in the car until the garage door closed. She sat still for another moment, despite Max nudging her with his nose.

"Wait!" she ordered her dog. "What if someone took over Elvin's house? The man could be tied up in a closet and we're walking into a trap."

The interior garage door opened revealing Elvin. "Why are you still sitting in the car?"

She blinked twice, then smiled at the appearance of her friend and swung her car door open. "I'm getting as paranoid as you. Once the garage door closed, I didn't know if I should worry that someone took over your house and lured me in."

"Good precaution. I should have at least texted you and told you it would be a garage entrance. My bad."

Here she thought her often joking friend would laugh at her paranoia. Instead, he accepted her excuse as reasonable. Huge topographic maps covered the garage walls. Some people might mistake it for hipster wallpaper but it wasn't. All his rooms displayed similar maps or graphs. Amy refused to stay there, insisting she felt like she was in M16, the British Intelligence Headquarters. The vaulting of Max from the car nudged her from her reverie.

"I came by to see what you had for me."

"Peculiar stuff. That's why I had you drive into the garage." He stepped away from the door, so she and Max could enter. They followed him to the kitchen where he gave Max a rawhide chew and grabbed a couple of cold drinks for them. "Let's go to the debriefing room."

Most people would call it the living room. The blinds were down and computer equipment crowded the room along with pieces from a sectional unit. Nala took a seat on one and Max the other. Elvin pointed to the kitchen. To her surprise, Max complied and padded to the next room.

"I really need *you* to train him."

"Ha! You spoil him. He's a reasonable dog."

She so wanted to disagree. Instead, she asked, "What's up?"

"I decided to take more precautions with my security." He shoved both hands into his pockets and paced the room. "I pride myself on not leaving any digital fingerprints, but I have the feeling someone is shadowing me."

"How do you know?" Elvin was her go-to guy when it came to spy technology and the dark web.

"Don't. It's just a feeling."

She gave a nod, not bothering to point out his various conspiracy theories. "Why did you have me…" She made a verbal correction when Max stuck his head around the door, "I meant us, come by?"

"I want to run some ideas past you." He took a seat in a rolling desk chair and popped his drink can open.

"You couldn't do this on the phone?" She held up her hand before Elvin could speak. "I know. Unsecured line."

"Big Brother could be listening in."

"Yes, I know." Sometimes, she was convinced Elvin had watched one too many spy movies or documentaries or something. "I need you to do a search on a guy while we talk. Magnus Lee McGee."

"Working," Elvin said, as he pivoted his chair to face the laptop and typed in the information. He scooted to another computer and did the same thing. "The other one is in the situation room. Be right back."

She watched him vanish into the hallway to work his magic on yet another computer. All these computers sucking down energy like a grade schooler eating candy surely would cause a spike of curiosity somewhere. Narcotics often found weed growers in ordinary homes due to their huge electric bills from grow lights being on twenty-four seven. When Elvin reappeared, she'd ask him.

"Okay," he came back rubbing his hands together. "I'm searching three databases."

"Couldn't I have done that?"

"Technically, yes, but no." He shook his head as he resumed his seat. "Before you ask and I know you will, one I actually pay to use and it's not cheap. A couple thousand a year. It's worth it. The other two are even pricier."

Nala whistled. "I had no clue you made so much."

"Digital security is important. I used a backdoor for the other two though."

"You hack into them?"

"When you say it, it sounds bad. I prefer *alternative* entrances." He pulled out a measuring tape from his pocket. "Let's measure the dog."

Max padded forward and placed his head in Elvin's lap to solicit petting. "You do realize if I couldn't get into these databases, I'd be no better than the guy who follows his ex through social media."

"Speaking of that…" Nala held her finger up. "My client told me Magnus had no social media presence. Isn't that odd?"

"Not necessarily. Depends on the man's age. While millennials might photograph and post everything they do, it isn't that popular with older men. Does your father have a social media presence?"

The idea made her laugh. "Dad? He'd call it a security risk. He's always warning his officers not to put up photos of themselves in uniform or even mentioning they're a police officer."

"Wow." Elvin wrote down a number on paper. "I thought *I* was paranoid."

"You are. Didn't I just enter through the garage?"

"I have legitimate reasons. If someone is hacking me why should you be in the spotlight, too?"

Even though Nala didn't buy into his theory, she did appreciate his thoughtfulness. An electronic chime sounded that had Elvin scooting to a monitor. "Did you check out this guy yourself?"

"No." She shrugged. "I thought there was no reason to since my client told me the police ran a scan on him and he was clean."

"Yeah, that's what I got here. Not even a parking ticket. Anything else you can tell me?"

Nala reviewed the conversation. "She said Magnus came from old money."

Instead of looking at his computer for confirmation, Elvin wrinkled his nose. "Seriously, guys are still using that line? Has she seen his old money mansion?"

"No mention of doing so. In fact, he's living with her."

Elvin shot one hand through his hair and said, "Unbelievable."

"What's unbelievable?" Nala scooted to the end of her seat feeling her initial unease returning.

"The crap some men get away with. If I said I came from old money, whatever girl I was trying to impress would pull out her smartphone and Google me. If no photo showed up of me in Images, I'd be history."

"I can see that with you." Nala steepled her fingers together. "I personally wondered why someone with money would choose to live in a cop's house. There won't be any of those fancy perks like jacuzzi tubs or home theatres."

Another electronic chime sounded causing Elvin to use his feet to scoot over to the other monitor. "Oh, I don't know about that.

What if the cop was dirty?"

Nala looked for something to throw at him. Finding nothing, she settled for a verbal reprimand. "Not funny."

"It happens."

"Not as much as crime dramas would have you believe. Besides, I have her address. Her neighborhood isn't as nice as yours."

Elvin turned and smirked. "I make more money than the average detective. They catch the bad guys after the crime happens. My job is to prevent the crime from ever happening." He glanced back at his monitor. "Nothing here. The guy must be a real boy scout. However, there's nothing under memberships, which is a red flag for me. He's not a member of anything."

"Why?" She never thought of not being a joiner to be a problem, it just meant you valued your alone time.

"Most organizations never take you off the roll. Anything from churches to bowling leagues keep all members on the roster. They can contact the person later for money. They also can brag about having two hundred members when only twenty ever show at one time. Sometimes, they get better pricing or preferential treatment with more members."

"I'm not in any clubs. Does that make me suspicious? I don't have time for that." She really didn't, especially now if she was going to do her job *and* Sawyer's.

The keyboard clicked underneath Elvin's rapid tapping. It made her wonder what he was doing. "Aha!" The man pressed one more key and the laser printer spat out a page, which he handed to Nala. "Not in any clubs, huh? I didn't take you for a line dancer."

"Lemon bars!" she murmured to herself as her eyes drifted down the names of various organizations and clubs. "I quit that health club years ago. Line dancing was Karly's idea. We only went twice. I'm still a member of Jazzy Combos? I don't believe it."

"Jazzy Combos," Elvin repeated the name. "It sounds like a snack. Should I ask?"

"No." She stuck out her tongue at Elvin. "It was college. I was trying to find myself. Didn't you do that at college?"

"There were no jazzy combos and…" A chime in the distance cut off whatever else he might say. He exited the room without finishing his sentence.

Just as well. Let him laugh at the various organizations she was supposedly a member of. While she might have applied to some on a whim, most she never joined. The only one she kept in contact with was Kappa Delta Pi, which was an educational honor sorority. It wasn't a party hard group, but more of a like-minded education group of students. Every now and then, she'd get a fund-raising call from the group. Surely, they knew what teachers made.

Elvin entered the room with furrowed brows. "I got nada on your guy. Maybe he's a stellar guy. But I have my doubts. No one is *that* clean."

Deidre wasn't asking for opinions, she just wanted facts. "Ok, that's all I need."

"I'm not satisfied, though." His lips pulled down in a frown. "I might continue to snoop on my own."

"That's not needed. Call me when you get the collar done." Nala stood, which caused Max to scamper to his feet.

"Already?" Elvin asked. "What's your hurry, sweetheart?"

Even though Elvin loved to do movie impressions, she had no

clue who they were nine out of ten times. "I have my job and apparently Sawyer's, too, until he comes back."

"How sweet you never lose hope in your partner." He patted her cheek the way an elderly aunt might treat a child.

"He'll come back." He had to. Wasn't that the whole plan behind sharing an office? If she wanted to play hardball, she *could* mention contractual obligations. Wait a minute. She never bothered to have a contract drawn up since she never thought this might happen. Not willing to hear any more, she headed to the door.

"Oh, by the way, there *was* another Magnus Lee McGee. He died about six months ago. Don't go off all mad. I still have to make Max's collar and something for you to wear to catch your Dog Park Romeo."

That ruined her huffy exit. "You do realize anything recorded can't be used in a court of law."

"I watched *Law and Order*." He waggled his eyebrows. "It's enough to convict someone. Most criminals will flip in a hurry if they think it will buy them less time. All we have to do is convince your culprit that we have the goods on him. No need to mention you only have two clients."

"Thanks, Elvin. I do have a clue how to do my job. Everyone wants to give me tips on how to be a private eye." Before, she just had the administration and the occasional parent who felt the need to tell her how to be a preschool teacher and on occasion, a student. Now, all and sundry were expert private eyes.

"Of course, they do," he agreed. "It's because you have a glamorous job."

Chapter Nine

A HORN HONKED in the distance. Another one answered. Sometimes, the city could be a bit like an urban symphony with all its varied sounds, especially in the mornings, with the rumble of garbage trucks and the low growl of the city buses making their rounds. Most of the time the noise energized her. It made her feel she was part of the bustle. Not today. She had too much on her mind.

She led Max around the corner and up the building steps without a word about the canine pulling on the leash. Part of her hoped Sawyer's talk about traveling the world with his friend would come to nothing. Haven't most people talked about seeing the world and never even left their own state? When she arrived at the office, he'd laugh about it and call it a crazy idea. The idea dropped her shoulders a little. She hadn't lost her office, yet.

With her first big case, she'd paid the rent a year in advance, but the year was almost gone. Many expenses she never anticipated, like the tall ceilings causing the electricity bill to be more than she expected, and advertising turning into an expensive necessity. People were not coming to her despite Karly handing out her business card with every dog or cat adopted. Apparently, most people adopting pets didn't have an immediate need for investigative services.

Inside the building, the sound of jazz music floated down the stairwell. It had to be Harry. She didn't have a radio in her office. Sawyer often used headphones, making it hard to know what he favored.

Harry's door stood open as she expected, allowing the music to spill out. *Odd.* Max must have thought so, too, since he stuck his nose into the office and barked.

"Max!" Harry's voice came from the backroom where he kept his inventory. He appeared, balancing a large stack of priority mail boxes. He set the unsteady stack on the desk. "I was heading out to the post office."

"I see. Lots of orders."

"Can't get anything past you," he teased. "I have to get everything out right away in time for Valentine's Day. I don't want to ruin anyone's evening if they don't get to dress up like Superman or Wonder Woman for their beloved."

"Ah." She hesitated, wondering if there was any right reply. "I know it's good business for you. I can't imagine anyone not showing up in costume for V-day. I'd be lucky to have *anyone* for V-day, showing up in costume or otherwise."

"Hear ya." He picked up half the stack and moved it into the hallway. "I've been meaning to ask if Karly said anything to you about me. I thought things were going well, but lately, she's as hard to catch as The Flash."

"Who?"

"Never mind. I mean about the Flash, not Karly."

She sucked in her lips, caught between two friends. Had Karly specifically told her not to say anything to Harry? "Well, I do know she likes you."

"That doesn't explain her not returning my calls or texts."

Nala wavered, not knowing if Karly would be thankful for her giving Harry the much-needed info. They were both her friends, although Karly had been her friend forever. Still, it would be nice if her friend could have a bit of romance in her life. "She's been very busy with the shelter. You know how she loves animals."

"I do." He gave a nod. "I've considered going down to the shelter and seeing what dogs they have available for adoption. I figure if you can bring your dog to work, I should be able to do likewise."

Max's ears pitched forward. Nala spoke quickly. "Partner. He's my partner."

"Yeah, I know that." He fixed his attention on the dog in question. "Sorry about that, Max." He brought his gaze back to Nala. "What about me getting a dog?"

"I think it's a win-win situation," she enthused.

A thoughtful expression crossed his face. "Do you think Karly would look favorably on my adopting a pet?"

"I know she will, *very* favorably."

Instead of replying, Harry carried the rest of his boxes out, pulled the door closed, grinned before stacking his boxes and headed down the stairs.

It was hard not to sigh, considering the man's enthusiasm. No doubt Karly and Harry would get back together, and she'd hear the patter of dog nails in the hallway soon. When she reached the third floor, the office was dark. Not a good sign. Sawyer always beat her to the office. He enjoyed working in the early hours, which never made sense to her, but sometimes their different schedules were beneficial. It allowed her to drop in to the office in the early evening without having to talk to Sawyer.

The man was like a stay-at-home mom who hadn't seen an actual adult for days. He always had a great deal to say. Still, she hesitated at the door, searching for her keys. If given a chance, she'd willingly listen to anything he had to say as long as he was on the other side of the door. She opened the door and pushed it ajar. "Search, Max."

Due to previous intruders, she was none too anxious to enter a dark office. Max barked once in the dark interior. Too bad he couldn't turn on the lights. She took three steps inside to reach for the light switch and regretted her habit of closing all the blinds before leaving. Even the weak winter light would be better than nothing.

A silhouette of a man stood in Sawyer's area.

"Sawyer?" She called out, wondering why the man would be in the dark, and clicked on the light. Instead of Sawyer, there was a cardboard cutout of a movie character. She let out her breath slowly, then laughed. It would have pleased Sawyer to know she'd mistaken Captain America for him. Being near the desk was peculiar. Normally, it resided against the back wall. A fluorescent note stuck out on the man's chest.

Obviously, she was meant to see it. She plucked the note off the spandex covered chest.

Dear Nala,

Had to leave sooner than I expected.

I would appreciate your help finishing the disability cases.

I labeled everything for you and told the company you'd invoice them.

The money is yours, of course.

Sawyer.

Brownies! She stomped her foot. That told her exactly nothing. Nothing about when he would be back or anything. She turned on a few more lights, then moved over to his computer. There were several files on top of the desk adorned with sticky notes detailing where he was on the case and who to forward the information to. *Great.*

It was time to get to work, but the question was should she start on her work or Sawyer's? First, she'd call Deidre. With the information Elvin gave her yesterday about there being an actual Magnus Lee McGee that had died, a face to face meeting she'd have to work into her schedule might be required.

She chose to use the landline. She was paying a monthly fee for the service, after all. It also had better clarity. Discreet didn't mean yelling results over a bad connection. She waited for the phone to ring.

"Deidre Williams."

"It's Nala." She didn't elaborate, especially with Deidre's suspicions that Magnus was reading her email. It would make sense that the man might be able to snoop on her phone, too. "Can you meet me for lunch?"

"Of course. Noon at our usual place?"

"Works for me." Nala answered under the impression that the usual place was her office.

"See you then."

She hung up and wondered if Magnus was spying on Deidre. Their conversation was vague enough not to cause alarm. After all, they never mentioned a place. Good friends would have a place they usually enjoyed that didn't necessarily need to be named. That ruined her plans to take Max on a lunch break walk at the dog park. Since it wasn't exactly around the corner, but in Broad Ripple, which would take a good thirty minutes both ways, it would be better if she made it an afternoon walk. With the sun being a pale imitation of its usual robust summer self, she'd better get there by three or she'd be in the dark.

Max nudged her hand resting in her lap. "Where's Sawyer?"

"Good question." She patted Max's dark head. "Somehow you missed the conversation yesterday."

He barked once, which sometimes served as laughter. "Please. You know all the human talk sounds alike. I only listen when words come up that interest me like food, cheeseburger, ride, walk, or danger."

"What about commands?" Most of the time, he obeyed.

"Goes without saying."

"Whatever. You'd think communicating with a dog who spoke English would be much easier."

Max gave her a narrow-eyed look, then moved across the room to lie down on the carpet. The silent treatment. It wasn't the first time he'd treated her to that. In truth, she usually got a lot of work done while Max was mad at her. It was going to be Sawyer's work until Deidre arrived. There wasn't that much involved in checking on people drawing disability. Usually, he checked the social media for photos of them doing physical things.

Most folks were smart enough not to upload photos of themselves dancing on the bar or water skiing when they were supposed to be recovering from a back injury. The same couldn't be said for their friends, who often tagged them. Sawyer had to do a screen capture before the post was removed.

He also did a little insurance loss work where people often claimed an object was stolen, then after the claim was paid, the object often reappeared. The stack included more than two dozen disability files. Macaroons! Didn't anyone actually work anymore?

The mindless work kept her relatively busy as she captured photos of one disability claimer bungee jumping. That was an activity she wouldn't do no matter what condition she was in.

The next case involved a pricy ruby necklace, which would mean combing through countless social media sites for a glimpse of the necklace. It would be easier to check out the kids' files. Even knowing they weren't supposed to talk about the necklace would be just enough incentive to do so. The file contained the name of the children. Nothing on the son—not that she expected much. A profile photo was posted of the daughter dressed up in an Arabian Nights, or something, costume. On her forehead was a big teardrop ruby. Nala checked the date of the image, then captured it. Someone was going to end up grounded.

The door glass rattled under a robust knock. It was either the police or Deidre.

Nala called out, "Come in!"

As the statuesque woman entered, Nala hurried out from behind Sawyer's desk. She definitely wanted to conduct this interview in her own office. Possibly sensing her plans, Max lunged up, gave a slow tail wag and a low *ruff.*

"This way." She led the way to the office. Deidre followed and took the client's seat and started talking.

"I was glad I could make it. We had some issues at work that made me wonder if I could get away, but I'm here now. What do you have?"

"As you know, there was no information on Magnus in the social media or newspapers. Not too surprising. There was another Magnus Lee McGee, but he died about six months ago."

She figured the bombshell would have a hardened narcotics officer show some surprise. The woman barely blinked. "Oh, that. Magnus told me about that. He's in the witness protection program."

"He told you that? When?" Better yet, why did she even bother with her investigation? Elvin was good, but she doubted even he could break through witness protection security.

"Last night." Deidre gave her a sly smile. "He didn't mean to tell me. Pillow talk, ya know."

It might have been pillow talk, but it came at an incredibly convenient time, just when his girlfriend was investigating him. "Should I assume you don't want me to dig any deeper?"

"That's right. I figured it would be better to tell you in person. I feel sorry about my suspicions now." She gave a laugh that sounded far from convincing.

"You're the client. You call the shots. No reason for me to go any further."

"Needless to say, I don't want any of my money back, and I'll recommend you to my friends." She stood up and wiggled her fingers. "Bye now."

Nala's stomach clenched as she watched the woman leave.

Something wasn't right, and Deidre wasn't that good of an actress, either. Nala waited until the door closed before she reached for her phone. She'd sworn she would never call Tyler Goodnight, but Deidre needed help.

A rich baritone came over the phone. "Nala."

"Yes, it's me. I think Deidre is in trouble. We need to talk."

"Do you want me to swing by the office?"

She glanced at her watch, calculating what was left of her day. "Meet me at Broad Ripple Dog Park around three-thirty."

"I'll be there with bells on."

"See ya." She hung up the phone.

Max quipped, "I can't wait to see what type of bells Officer Goodnight will be wearing."

"Me, too."

Chapter Ten

A STIFF WIND swept through the leafless trees, chilling Nala. She pulled her coat closer. No wonder there were very few people in the dog park. Add in that it was a weekday and neither noon nor after work when most people would bring their dogs.

She made a show of fussing over Max's collar, the one Elvin had modified, while she checked out the other park visitors. Elvin had wanted to use a camera that resembled a Christmas tree ornament hanging from his collar as if that wouldn't attract attention. Then, he'd wanted Nala to wear something similar, preferably on her chest, where he figured most men would look, giving the camera a chance for good identification. The plan might have worked, except it was winter. They settled on a decorative pin camera fastened to her coat. It was ugly, but if anyone asked about it, she would say it a was gift from one of her students.

"Okay, Max, I want you on your good behavior."

He answered in a low voice. "What does that mean? I'm always good."

Actually, he wasn't but he was probably better than most dogs. "Well, first of all, you need to bark, not talk. Act like a dog, but try not to frighten anyone, such as that little old lady over there with the two tiny terriers."

"The two tiny terriers," Max echoed her words. "I wonder if I can say that fast. Two tiny terriers. Tiny two terriers."

"Stop. Officer Max, you are now on duty." She knew the command her father used when working with canines would snap her dog into form. He stopped talking, and his visage took on alertness, as opposed to his earlier silly expression. "I will walk you around the grounds. Today, you will remain on the leash so the possible suspect can approach us."

They took a slow stroll, nodding at fellow dog owners, but not smiling. There was an older man with an equally as old basset hound, not too surprisingly. Those who came out in the middle of the day were retired or on third shift work. A few might work from home. A young blonde woman in a full-length coat walked a Löwchen. Nala recognized the long-haired dog because Karly once got one in at the shelter and mentioned they could cost as much as ten thousand dollars. She had studied the image on Karly's phone trying to decide why one dog would cost so much more than others. Whatever the reason, it hadn't stopped it from ending up at the shelter.

Trophy wife—Nala automatically labeled the blonde. She was probably a former model and now graced the arm of her much older, rich husband. A man in the far corner of the park had a schnauzer. The middle-aged man wearing wire-rim glasses did not look like the type to sweet talk a woman out of thousands of dollars. When he caught her staring, he immediately glanced away. The action struck her as the actions of a shy person. He probably bought the dog for companionship, not that she could judge. She'd done about the same with Max. She'd had no high hopes that he'd guard her home or help with her case workload.

A handsome man with dark hair, wearing a leather jacket with a muffler tucked around his neck, strolled in with a rottweiler on a tight leash. *Maybe.* One of the women described him as a young Mark Harmon. Unfamiliar with the actor, she'd googled him. The actor did have a nice smile and dark hair when he was younger. The second woman had mentioned dark hair. So far, handsome and mysterious had checked all the boxes. He noticed her interest and smiled.

Fudge! He noticed her eyeing him. Not good. She looked away, pushed back a tendril of hair, and led Max in the opposite direction, even though the dog park wasn't huge, and people were bound to stumble across each other. With her back to the man, she considered his appearance. Physically, he matched the women's description of a handsome man with dark hair. They said he was young or younger, which would have translated to younger than them. She needed another look to gauge his age, but she needed to play it cool.

Apparently, Dog Park Romeo didn't approach women who were too friendly. That's why the previous foray in the park with Karly wouldn't have amounted to anything. Karly had the hopeful puppy face that yelled *please like me.* She'd also try to make contact with every likely man and smile at him.

Nala's clients were not flirts. One was a businesswoman, the other a recent widow.

A turn was coming up that would give her a chance to see the majority of the park, and she'd be able to judge the newcomer's age. It was a good thing she came to the park early. By the time Tyler showed up she might even be asked out by the con man.

A slight turn of the head found the man in question staring back at her. Nala snapped her eyes ahead as the man in question made his way over to her.

"Hello, I'm Hunter," he offered and flashed his beautiful smile again.

"I'm Nala."

Under different conditions, she might even have considered the man hot. Now, he was possibly a slimy bottom feeder who preyed on tender-hearted, dog-loving women.

"Just the dedicated dog lovers out in this weather."

She gave a short nod, trying not to appear too interested. Dog Park Romeo preferred his women to be a little more of a challenge, or at least that's what she assumed. None of her clients admitted to being easily swayed, but then who would, especially after being tricked?

Not discouraged, he gestured to Max while his own dog pulled at the lead, obviously having no interest in his owner's conversation. Still in duty mode, Max stood without moving with ears perked forward and ready to spring into action if the situation warranted it.

"He looks like a good dog."

"He is." She said as little as possible and only halfway looked at him. Strong profile, great hair, nice smile, he probably had those melting liquid eyes, too. No reason to chance it, although she'd have to look at him if they did go on a date. Otherwise, he'd leave, thinking she was weird and not a good bet as far as soliciting money for his ailing pooch.

The pooch in question continued to tug at the leash, causing Mr. Smooth to lose his confident pose as he stumbled, then jerked on the leash. "Raider, stop it!"

Instead of complying, the dog gave a strong bark. Nala put her hand up to her face to hide her initial desire to laugh at the man's discomfort. It could scare him off. Even though Max was doing his best at-rest stance, even he barked. A welcoming bark, which meant someone she knew was headed their way.

It had to be her mother. No matter how much she tried to discourage her parent, her mother was determined to help. It was unfortunate she'd mentioned the name of the dog park. It didn't mean the man limited himself to one park. She inhaled deeply to smother a sigh. Her mother would ruin it.

Hunter turned to see who the dogs were barking at and he sighed. "Good Lord, I should have known."

It was hard to miss Tyler in his full uniform striding across the snow-dusted grass with a determined expression. Obviously, Max didn't, and he gave another delighted bark while the rottweiler broke free and ran toward Tyler, who knelt and embraced the dog.

Of course, all dogs would love him. The man beside her grumbled something. Why would he be upset in the presence of the law? Now he'd retreat without her finding anything out about him or making a date. Fig bars! A quick glance at her watch indicated Tyler was much earlier than they agreed on. He belly-rubbed the happy rottweiler, then glanced up at the man.

"This is what you do with your off-time, accost women in the park?"

Hunter snorted, then turned his attention to Nala. "Was I accosting you?"

"No, not at all." Apparently, Tyler knew the man, which meant he wasn't her guy. They might even be friends or worse, co-workers. Not afraid of falling under a con man's spell, she gave the man a more thorough look. He'd left her side to regain his dog. His hair was a close, neat cut favored by the police. He had more bangs than her father would approve of, but possibly kept that hidden with his cap.

That was no good. So far, hanging out at dog parks hadn't landed her any suspects. All she had so far was grudging respect for owners who drove their pets to the park.

With some slaps on the back, laughter, and an, "Oh, I see," from Hunter, he gathered up his dog and left. What was that all about?

Max nudged her leg until she squatted beside him to hear his whisper. "Am I still on duty?"

"No, I guess not."

He took advantage of her loose hand on the lead and darted toward Tyler as the previous dog had done. A charging shepherd could easily knock a person down, but Max skidded to a halt beside the man. The tilt of the head told her he was looking up at the man adoringly. He probably thought Tyler had a cheeseburger in his pocket.

They strolled up to her. Max sat while Tyler gave her a wink. "Good thing I showed up when I did with Hunter putting the moves on you."

"Yeah, good thing," she agreed but wondered if it really was. Her goal had been not to date a cop. She'd seen and lived with the demands a cop's family had to endure, but all she seemed to attract was cops. It had to be the dog.

"What did you want to talk to me about?" Tyler inquired.

Ah yes, there was a reason for his being there. She made a careful survey of the park. The lady with the two tiny terriers was gone as was the trophy wife. Only Basset Hound Man remained. The man and his dog were on a bench sharing a snack. No one was close enough to overhear.

"I'm worried about Deidre. Her boyfriend isn't who he says he is. He has a dead man's social security number, which is probably why you didn't find a criminal history."

Tyler's amused expression slipped as he took off his hat and ran his hand through his hair. "I ran the check myself. Deidre asked me to. It would have mentioned if the man was deceased."

"It would have if you ran it after he died, possibly not natural causes. When I presented the information to Deidre, she insisted her boyfriend was in the witness protection program."

He shook his head and replaced his hat. "Why didn't she tell us that in the first place?"

Max, bored with the conversation, lay down on the chilly ground. Nala cleared her throat to explain. "She didn't know until last night when Magnus told her. Personally, I think he purposely let it slip in an intimate moment. Sounds too convenient to me. He knew she was getting suspicious or looking into it, so he makes up the witness protection thing. I'm afraid Deidre wants to believe it badly enough that she closed the case."

"Not good when Deidre is heading up a sting operation."

So many things could go wrong when an officer allowed emotions to overrule logic. She hoped Deidre wasn't doing that. "I can continue to check into Magnus, but someone needs to alert narcotics."

"Easier said than done." Tyler put a closed fist to his lips as he thought. He dropped his hand and gave a heavy sigh. "I could talk to Deidre, which would alert her, and could eventually get back to the boyfriend. I'll go see what I can do."

"I appreciate it. I'll call you as soon as I get more information."

"You do that." He made a half-turn as if he were moving toward the squad car, then turned back. "I didn't come here for Deidre. Sure, I care about her as a fellow officer. I came because of you." He reached for her gloved hand. "I realize we had a lot of false starts as far as us dating. I'd like to try again if you would."

This wasn't expected, but she had hoped, a little. Make that a lot. "I would."

Max barked, adding his agreement.

Chapter Eleven

TYLER HAD JUST announced he'd like to try dating again after an awkward history of misunderstandings and possibly overexuberant parents on Nala's part. Her mother's inexplicable need for a grandchild and her father's desire for the son he never had come together to create a perfect storm. Instead of a blizzard or a hurricane, with her parents, it resulted in a little matchmaking. Any unexpected invitation to dinner or an event could result in an eligible man who had somehow been tricked into attending, too.

A snowflake lazily drifted down to rest on the bill of Tyler's uniform cap. He *did* look nice, even holiday movie-worthy. She sucked in her lips to keep from blurting out her thoughts. Graham, her father, never made any secret of his preference for Tyler. Both she and her mother joked that the two had a bromance going on, which abruptly ended when the old girlfriend showed up. Even though she chose not to investigate the matter, it wasn't as easy for her parents, who refused to let go of Tyler. Sometimes, she joked they loved him more than her.

Of course, he was on the force. In that area, her father respected his choice to join the honorable legacy of peace officers, whereas she became an investigator, despite all the early training her father insisted on giving her. By age nine, she could outshoot her classmates, bluff all her contemporaries at go fish, and was an expert eyewitness.

A smile blossomed, and her heart expanded as she contemplated giving Tyler another try. This time she tried not to get ahead of herself.

Her gloved right hand was still clasped in his left. The dog park was almost empty, and Max sat nearby leaning slightly on Tyler. As canines went, Max was never shy to show his affection. Her eyes met his twinkling gaze.

"I'm good about the dating, but I have one condition."

He pushed the brim of his hat up as if not to miss anything and arched one eyebrow. "Does it have anything to do with keeping Max supplied in cheeseburgers?"

Nothing was wrong with his memory. It made her question if he remembered her idiosyncrasies as well. She hoped not. The thought made her nose wrinkle. "Nope. You couldn't afford to keep him in cheeseburgers. Besides, he's spoiled as it is. I would love to get to know you better on my own."

His brows knitted together, and he removed his hat to scratch his head. "Before I came by, I was talking to my partner about female doublespeak. Since Kevin is married, he's an expert on the subject. He explained that often women say one thing and mean another. A smart man knows the code. I would have thought us going out would give you a chance to get to know me and possibly clear up some misperceptions your parents have about me."

"Yeah." She nodded. "Most people would think that, but they don't have Graham and Gwen Bonne as parents."

"*Oh.*" He emphasized the word. "Got it." He winked. "It would have been nice to let Captain Bonne know things were good between us. He's been breathing down my neck wondering what I did to sour things between us."

"What!" The idea of her father taking advantage of his position to grill Tyler had her dropping the leash and pulling her hand from his. She raised both hands in horror. "I can't believe this. It's so unprofessional. You could file a grievance against him."

He gave a short laugh. "You probably recalled I did some work at Hamilton County for a while." He cleared his throat. "It was right after our misunderstanding. I thought it would help to put some distance between myself and your father. He was the one who asked me to come back to IPD. The pay was better and I knew the other officers, which made it a no brainer. I would never say anything against your father. Never mind, I was exaggerating." He held up one gloved finger. "I'd be more than happy to honor your request if you promised to say nothing to your father."

"Done." She held her hand to shake. Tyler took it and gave it a firm shake. In the distance, she heard a familiar bark. A downward glance revealed that Max was no longer at her feet. "Brownies!"

The exclamation caused him to chuckle. "I've missed both of you." Tyler pointed to the shy man she had labeled earlier in her initial foray of the park. The man had his dog in his arms and was slowly backing away from Max.

Nala cupped both hands around her mouth and yelled. "He's friendly!"

"You know he's not going to believe that." Tyler whistled and slapped his leg.

Max turned and ran toward him with enthusiasm. Why didn't Max show similar energy when she called him? Maybe familiarity did breed contempt. She grabbed the leash when he came closer. "You're going to get me kicked out of the dog park."

Not even an apologetic look. Instead, he let Tyler pull off a glove and scratch him behind the ears just the way he liked. Good heavens, her dog was easy. If Officer Goodnight threw in a cheeseburger, it was possible Max might decide to relocate.

"You're ruining my dog. He did something wrong and shouldn't be rewarded."

Tyler stopped scratching Max to respond. "You dropped the leash. He didn't run away or chase anything. All he did was wander up to the only dog in the park. He probably wanted to play."

"Probably. With his being as big as he is, people assume he wants to eat their dog half the time."

"Poor guy." Tyler fondled Max's ears. "Technically, I'm on a late lunch. I'll grab something as I head back." He reached up to fix his hat. "One more thing…" He took her hand and held her gaze.

Here it comes—*the kiss*. Should she close her eyes? If she did, that would mean she expected to be kissed. It would be better to act surprised. She waited, her heart beating a little faster than when she arrived at the park. Her eyelids dropped a little, ready to close if need be. It was just awkward staring at someone close up.

His head was angled slightly to hers as he spoke. "I know Deidre told you the case was closed."

This was not what she expected. The eyelids snapped up. "Um, okay."

"I realize as an investigator and with Elvin's assistance, you can get information much quicker than going through official channels. I'd count it a favor if you continued the investigation, and I would pick up the bill, too."

"Nothing might come of it." Never mind that Deidre would be mad. "Not sure if this is on the level."

He made a derisive snort. "You're kidding me. Didn't you hear me say that you and Elvin can do things the police can't?"

"I heard you. I'm not deaf." The warm, happy feeling was morphing into irritation. Tyler was a pleasure to look at, which almost made her forget the rivalry that sometimes existed between cops and investigators. Never mind that many retired cops turned *into* investigators. "You have your own tools and experts. Why not use them?"

His hand went up to hold his cap in place as he lifted his face to the cloudy sky and spoke to it as opposed to her. "I thought about it. Only for a minute. Maybe Deidre's boyfriend is dirty. Love can be blind, but I don't think Deidre is, at least not forever. If we can find the needed information and present it to her, then we can get ahead of this situation before it blows up on her. No way other officers wouldn't believe she was involved. Even if she wasn't indicted by the judicial system, she would be by other officers. Technically, she might keep her job, but it wouldn't be in narcotics. You might see her writing out parking violations and driving that glorified scooter around."

"I see." It was a long stretch from the kiss she anticipated. "What if Magnus is under witness protection?"

He lowered his gaze from the sky to meet her eyes. A frosty puff came from his mouth as he spoke. "Do you think he's just an ordinary guy hopelessly in love with Deidre?"

"Nope, too secretive, too suspicious, and he checks her phone and email. If nothing else, he's way too possessive. At best, he'd be an uncomfortable boyfriend to have."

A grunt served as an answer. An electronic squawk sounded, then a code call came on the radio. "Code 26."

Since her father made her practice the codes, Nala identified it. "Gunshot."

Tyler sighed. "Not sure why Deidre is so dead set on this guy." He angled his head, pushed the button on the radio and spoke into it. "Received and responding." He reached out and cradled her cheek before turning and jogging to his vehicle.

"He wonders why Deidre is so determined to hold onto her guy. As far as I can tell, single men aren't thick on the ground," she grumbled.

Max surged to his feet, making a survey of the empty park. "I don't see any males on the ground."

"Never mind." Sometimes, she tried to explain sayings to her dog, but it didn't take long for her to realize Max tended to take everything literally. "We're done. I might need to google dog parks."

They strolled in the direction of her car, a vintage beetle. A rumble of a heavy vehicle and a slight grinding of gears made her think school bus or garbage truck. The sight of a blue sanitation truck confirmed her second guess. It also alerted her how close to the dumpster she had parked, which didn't seem like the best option right then. Why had she ever thought it was a smart move? The metal arms went out to embrace the unwieldy dumpster and barely missed her car.

"Macaroons!" She moaned and closed her eyes. It was too close for comfort. A horrendous crash had Max erupting into his frenzied barking. The blue dumpster sat on top of her car or what was left of it. The sanitation truck driver peered out, then reversed the truck, and aimed the front of the truck toward the parking lot exit. He was making a run for it after destroying her only mode of transportation.

"Stop!" she yelled to no effect. The man didn't hear her or pretended not to. The truck lumbered away. How could she stop it? It wasn't like she could run along beside the vehicle yelling citizen's arrest. Her mother had gifted her with a portable siren she swore every woman needed to carry. It might even make the driver think actual police were on their way. He should at least pull to the side.

She dropped the leash and pawed through her crowded purse, searching for the siren while keeping her eyes on the truck. The strap broke on her purse spilling out the contents. She made an effort to grab the contents, but most spilled out, including her weapon, which she had almost grabbed before it landed with a hard thump, sending a bullet whizzing toward her car.

A flash, then an explosion knocked her down and sent Max fleeing. Her head hit the pavement, and everything went black.

Chapter Twelve

THE EXPLOSION KNOCKED Nala flat on her back. Sirens sounded in the distance. The cold pavement chilled her cheek as a heaviness pinned her to the ground. Her heart raced as a fluttery sensation filled her stomach. Breathing took concentration as she reminded herself to take air in and out. What had happened? A single bullet should not have blown up her car, but it had. Shooting a weapon in a public place could either get her slapped with a misdemeanor or felony, depending on her intention. Her only intention was to find her tiny siren.

"Ma'am, ma'am, are you, all right?"

She blinked. Her vision went in and out of focus, similar to when she sat in the dark behind an optometrist machine that made letters intentionally blurry. No, not okay. Not okay by a long shot. Her car just exploded. A bullet couldn't ignite a gas tank unless it was a tracer round. She remembered that from watching that myth debunking show. Even if she hadn't watched the show, her father was always pointing out things in both movies and television that could not happen. Sometimes, he'd even mute the show to explain why.

The image of the hard-hatted sanitation worker came into view. It meant she wasn't dead. If she was, Heaven needed an upgrade on their angels and their heating system. The significance of the person leaning over her coalesced in her slow working mind. She tried to jerk upright, but her head throbbed so much she slid back to the cold ground as the rumble and squeal of emergency vehicles reverberated inside her head. Nala managed to raise an accusatory finger. "You! You killed my car."

"Not intentionally," the man started, only to be interrupted by a paramedic.

"Who's been injured?"

The sanitation worker backed up to reveal Nala. A uniformed woman knelt on the ground beside her. "Do you think anything is broken?"

"I don't know. The explosion knocked me down."

"Explosion?" A uniformed fireman came up behind the paramedic and repeated the word. "I guess that's what started the fire."

The paramedic shot the fireman an undecipherable look but continued running her hands over Nala's body while inquiring if anything hurt. So far, Nala knew her head hurt, an elbow, a knee, and her foot were extra cold. She twisted her body enough to see her shoeless foot. "Where's my boot?"

"Can't say." The paramedic eased her back down and checked her eyes with a penlight. "I'd say that's enough evidence of an explosion. People lose their shoes when the igniting force spreads outward and throws them for a loop. Be glad that's all you lost."

"I loved those ankle boots." Her voice sounded weak and somewhat whiny. Her father never tolerated whininess and did his best to discourage such behavior. She squeezed her eyes shut, steeling herself to be strong. Something on the edge her memory needed to be recalled. What was it? Her thoughts were playing hide and seek with her. They were there one minute, then gone when she tried to verbalize them.

"Max!" She tried to sit up, despite the throbbing at the back of her head. Her dog was missing. Where was he? "I have to find my dog."

"Miss! You need to calm down first," the paramedic urged. "Animal control can find your dog."

"No, no, not that!" It would be horrible for a dog that had been sent to the pound so often to end up there again. No guarantee he'd end up at the shelter where Karly was. "I have to find my dog."

The strobing of the emergency lights lit up the area in the approaching twilight. Even though it had been threatening to snow heavily all day, the clouds chose that exact minute to let loose their crystalline treasure. Big, wet snowflakes danced in the sky, giving the fire officers who were putting out her car fire a surreal image, almost like someone had photoshopped a Christmas card image over a news photo.

The pounding of running feet vibrated through the ground and her body. Why did everything have to hurt so much? Colors exploded behind her closed eyelids.

"Nala! Nala!" A breathless Tyler slid to a stop and flashed his badge to the paramedic. "Officer Goodnight, I heard the call on the radio. How is she?"

"Nothing appears to be broken. A possible concussion. Are you a family member?"

Tyler was here. He'd do something about Max. She reached out her hand toward him. His gloved hand met hers. "Find Max."

"I'm worried about you. Let me notify your father at least."

Even now Max could be running for his life or hurt. "Max, first."

"Okay, but we need to take care of you." He nodded at the paramedic. "Not a family member, but I do know her family. Nala Bonne. Her father is police captain, Graham Bonne, who I'm calling right now."

He spoke into his radio. "At the scene. There's a victim."

"Not the radio," she begged. It would not serve to have her name mentioned on police scanners. Her mother had one in her office, and the last thing she wanted was for her mother to hear her only child was being rushed to the hospital. After all, she wasn't really hurt, just shook up. She pushed to her elbows and peered into the darkening park. All she had to do was stand up. Then she could find Max.

Tyler continued. "Female. On route to Broad Ripple Dog Park. Okay, you heard. Can you have Captain Bonne call me ASAP? Officer Goodnight, out."

A metallic clank near her head announced the arrival of a gurney. A male paramedic nodded at his partner. "We need to get her on a backboard and secure her neck with a cervical collar."

"Copy." The woman paramedic replied, then addressed Nala with a sympathetic smile. "I know you think you're fine, but it's best to have everything checked out. Besides the obvious injuries, you could have internal injuries. By the way, my name is Mary. I should have told you that at first."

She heard the woman speaking or at least part of her did. The other part strained to hear whatever Tyler was saying as he held his cell phone up to his mouth. It had to be her father. "Tell him I'm okay."

A lone bark came from the direction of a copse of trees. "Max! Go get Max. He's over there." She gestured to where she thought the bark came from. Her hand flopped around as if it wasn't really responding to her need. At least, not in a manner she'd like.

Tyler ended the call and hovered close to Nala who was having a backboard carefully moved under her. "Your father will meet you at the hospital. I imagine your mother will be there, too. I forgot to ask."

Had he even heard her when she asked him to get Max? It took so much concentration and effort to form words. Maybe she could send him psychic messages, though not sure why that would work when they often couldn't accomplish decent verbal communication at times. Another bark sounded causing Tyler to look away. He put his fingers up to his mouth and managed an ear-splitting whistle that made her head hurt even more.

A black dog ran out of the darkness, startling a few emergency workers in the process. He skirted the smoldering car and came to stand beside the gurney, which was still collapsed at ground level. His long, canine tongue swiped her face, and he whimpered.

Nala managed to entwine her fingers into the fur around his neck. It smelt smoky, and dried blood was on his snout. "He's hurt."

The paramedics threaded the cervical collar under her neck and snapped it in place, which didn't allow much movement, especially when attached to the backboard. She just had to assume the people she saw previously were still around her.

"Tyler…" she croaked his name, feeling drained by the event. It was hard to keep her eyes open, and she wasn't sure if she needed to or not. Mary had told her she didn't have a concussion or was that she might have a concussion? So hard to remember.

"I'm here." Tyler rushed to the other side of the gurney where she could see him. In his hand was the end of Max's trailing leash.

"Take care of Max."

"I will."

The two paramedics took opposite ends of the gurney and popped it up to its full position, ready to roll. "Kiss her goodbye," Mary suggested. "We need to get her to the hospital right now."

What a bossy paramedic to assume so much about her and Tyler! Surprisingly, he did dust a kiss on her forehead and whispered. "I'll see you soon. Got to go get Max checked out."

Of course, he will. A man she could depend on. That's what he was. Her eyelids fluttered closed on their own, which was just as well because exhaustion sucked her under. Despite a shaking of her shoulders and an entreaty for her to stay with them, she couldn't.

Chapter Thirteen

AN ANTISEPTIC ODOR irritated Nala's nose, and a nurse bustled around, spreading cold, medical goo on her body and attaching wires to it. In a matter of seconds, there was a rhythmic chorus coming from the monitors. Her hours watching medical dramas paid off by letting her know her beeps sounded normal. No reason to call the crash cart yet.

A middle-aged man going silver at the temples and with a lab coat over his street clothes came into the room and stood at the end of her bed. Did they send out for central casting for him? The doctor checked the various machines that recorded her vital signs and murmured under his breath. He questioned the attending nurse, then addressed Nala.

"You are a very fortunate young woman."

That wasn't exactly her opinion. Hadn't her car just exploded, and she was in the hospital being poked and probed? Only earlier today, she thought things were looking up, especially when she and Tyler tentatively made plans to date. Her hand went up to finger the back of her head. Needles of pain shot up her arm. "Ouch!"

The doctor gave a sage nod. "Inflammation." He made a note on the electronic tablet he was carrying. "We're going to x-ray it."

How long was she going to be here? She needed to see Max. The door was ajar, allowing her to hear voices in the hall and the distant wail of an ambulance. There was the squeak of wheels, possibly a gurney or a wheelchair.

Her mother's voice cut through the other hallway sounds. "Where's my daughter? Don't shush me. I have a right to be here. Graham, show them your badge."

Nala's shoulders relaxed, allowing her head to sink down into the flimsy excuse for a pillow. Her mother might be difficult, competitive, and a bit of a know it all, but she was Nala's biggest champion. Whatever Nala needed, Gwen would make it happen. The only real problem was she and her mother had vastly different ideas about what she needed. Right now, she needed to leave. Still, it would be amusing to see the doctor's reaction to her opinionated parent.

Her mother pushed into the room and was at Nala's side in a heartbeat.

"Ma'am, you're not supposed to be in here," the nurse tried, but was pinned like a butterfly by a collector by one of her mother's imperious looks.

"I am her mother. A girl needs her mother." Her mother uttered the words with certainty. The unspoken part was *and nothing else will serve*. Nala heard that part echo in her head even if the others didn't.

Her father waved from the doorway giving the medical staff some room to move. "Hello, princess."

"Dad." Here she thought her mother would be the one to embarrass her. "I'm okay."

The doctor was attempting to get her mother to leave. "Say

goodbye. I'll be out after the tests to tell you what's happening and the course of treatment we will pursue."

The course of treatment? That didn't sound right. "You told me I was a very fortunate young lady."

"You are," he agreed. "You're fortunate to be alive and have all your limbs attached, especially after that explosion."

"About that explosion," her father queried and took a step closer. He ignored the doctor, but pulled out his badge and flashed it in the man's direction. "I'm a concerned parent, naturally, but there could be a domestic terrorist loose in our city. You're going to have to allow this."

The red-faced doctor stood with his mouth open. It was probably one of the few times since he donned his white coat that someone hadn't listened to him.

Her father leaned forward and kissed her cheek while her mother held onto two fingers of her right hand where the IV needle had been placed.

"Nala, I need you to think back about everything you remember before the explosion."

Some grumbling came from the doctor and a threat to call security. Graham held up his hand. "This will only take a second. If we can get the misfit who did this off the streets, my daughter will be safe. The sooner it is done, the better. Even the hospital is at risk if we don't. I'm pretty sure you don't want some village idiot with a pipe bomb to show up in your emergency room?"

Instead of answering, the doctor stepped back as her father continued. "Start with your morning."

"I tried to get into work early. I found out Sawyer was gone. I went over the work he wanted me to finish." Her mind searched for opportunities when someone could have attached a bomb to her car. The car was sitting in her driveway all night. She'd have to start putting it in the garage. Wait, she didn't have a car anymore. She groaned. No car equaled no transportation, which made it hard to be an investigator. How would she get to the dog parks?

"Damn peculiar." Her father's brows beetled into a V as he spoke.

"The explosion?" She might have used a stronger word than *peculiar*.

"No." He shook his head slowly. "Too bad, Sawyer took off. You could have used the help."

Despite being peeved with her office mate, she felt the need to defend him. "He had no way of knowing my car would blow up."

"Did he, or didn't he?"

Oh great, it was his *everybody is a suspect* attitude. Nala had been grilled by her father many times. It was usually enough to have her admitting to any wrongdoing, often bringing up things she had done in the past. "Sawyer is on a plane heading to who knows where. Someplace with exotic women with lovely accents, I guess."

"What happened after you did the slacker's work?"

Nala felt she should object to the term *slacker*, but she had used it in her head, too. "I had a client come in. It was one of those date search things. I gave her my intriguing results, and she asked me to call off the check."

Her father gave her a long stare. He expected her to tell him the results. "Dad, it's confidential. I do discreet inquiries."

"Could be the boyfriend objected to what you found out and decided to put you out of business permanently."

"Graham," Her mother reached across Nala's body to poke her husband. "You're talking to our only child, not one of your street thug informants."

"Gwen." He pulled back enough to be out of range of his wife's hands. "I know who I'm talking to, and I'm trying to keep our only child safe. To do that, I need information."

Geesh. Having her parents squabble over her prone body was another thing she hadn't planned to do today. "I don't think it was her boyfriend because she was super cautious. Still, let me talk to Tyler about it, and I'll get back to you."

"Tyler, Tyler Goodnight?" her mother asked, back to holding Nala's index and middle fingers.

"This would work better if I was the one asking questions. Be quiet and nurturing."

Unfortunately, her mother's grip tightened at the words. "Mom! Ease up. You know Dad doesn't mean anything by it. It's who he is."

Gwen loosened her grip but shot her husband a look. "Instead of putzing through her penny ante cases, maybe you should look at your own cases. If one of those jokers you put behind bars wanted to get at you, it would be easier to get to your daughter."

Nala expected another repeat of hush and nurture. Instead, her father's eyes rolled upward. "You have a point. I'll have to check to see who has been released, not that it would mean anything. A few have the ability to pull strings behind bars, too."

Lemon bars! She always considered her father a touch paranoid with his emergency drills and hostage training. She was the only grade schooler who knew how to get out of a car trunk if locked in. Her father was the king of worst-case scenarios, but he had made them into a game. All the time, he was training her to survive, just in case the worst happened. Had it? "Dad, do you think—?" She left the question hanging.

"I don't know, sweetheart. We have the bomb squad looking into what is left of the car. Portable searchlights had been brought in to search for debris. The snow isn't helping, though." His lips pulled down into a pronounced frown and he shook his head. "What about your client?"

She pursed her lips together. In her investigative training, she'd been warned that the police might try to shake her down for information. According to the course, she didn't have to tell them anything unless they had a warrant. What she hadn't expected was her father would be doing the asking. "I'll need to talk to Tyler first."

"Why him? Why is Officer Goodnight involved in everything today?" Her father straightened from his crouching position and folded his arms.

She recognized that position. As a teenager, it'd sometimes had her knees knocking, especially if she'd been up to something forbidden. Too bad for him. It wasn't going to work today. "The client is Tyler's friend, and he should be able to talk to her discreetly."

"She's a cop?" Graham demanded. "Then I absolutely should know what is happening."

Nala closed her eyes as she worked on arranging her face into the poker mask she'd practiced in the mirror. "Not necessarily."

"Girlfriend?" her mother asked.

"No." She answered without thinking. "Would you like to hear about the rest of my day? The part with the explosion?"

"Go ahead." He circled his hand for her to continue.

"As you know, I haven't had much luck with Dog Park Romeo. Elvin created a collar for Max that would transmit everything to a recorder while I had a pin on my coat that functioned as a camera. We had both on when we went to the park."

"That's it!" Her father slapped his hands together. "I need the pin and the transmission records. Where's Max?"

Maybe Max wasn't his favorite child after all. "Tyler was taking him to the vet."

"Tyler, Tyler, Tyler. Where was Officer Goodnight when the explosion happened?"

So much for keeping any possible dating activity on the QT. "He had just left. We agreed to meet at the park, then there was a call about a gunshot that he needed to respond to."

"Makes me wonder if it was meant to pull the officer away from you. Of course, anyone who knows you should know you're an accurate and deadly shot, too."

"Graham," Her mother covered her face with her spread fingers. "I hope you don't talk about Nala like that to everyone."

"Why not? I'm proud." He directed a teasing smile at Nala.

Sometimes, her brilliant father missed the obvious, but it was more likely he enjoyed pulling his wife's chain. "Dad, she's afraid you're scaring off my dating prospects with talk of my deadly accuracy with a pistol."

"Not sure why that would be off-putting. You don't need a man who can't shoot as well as you anyhow. The transmissions?"

She pounded on the bed railing with her free hand, causing the vibration to travel up her arm. "The receiver was in my car! What else can go wrong? Still, Elvin usually has backup systems. Take the pin and collar to Elvin and see what he can download. Be nice to

Tyler when you see him."

"I'm always nice," her father insisted.

Her mother held up an index finger. "You think you're being nice, but sometimes you overwhelm people. Keep it cool."

"Okay, everyone." The doctor waved his arms as if he were trying to shoo geese. "Your time is up."

Graham glared at the man, then placed a hand on his chest as he addressed Nala. "I will chill for you, princess. I'll be back to see how you are. I left your bag by the door. Where's the coat you had on?"

"Ask the nurse, she helped me get undressed and into this drafty gown."

The woman in question stepped away from the wall to assist her father. Her mother patted Nala's hand. "I was at home when your father called. I figured you would need clothes, possibly pajamas, and toiletries and packed you a bag."

She would need all of the above. "Did you stop by my house?"

"No worries about your house not being clean. I got the clothes from your old bedroom." She gave the fingers a little squeeze. "Good thing I held onto that stuff."

"What stuff?" Anything worth taking, she had taken with her when she moved out. Normally, her designer mother did updates to each room, but little had happened to hers. It served as a shrine to her teenage years when she left for college. Later, she hadn't taken down the posters of the various boy bands or the kitten hanging by one paw reminding her to hang in there, because it amused her. It was also a passive-aggressive attempt to see how long it would take for her mother to turn the room into a magazine-worthy spread. It had never happened.

Gwen's heels tapped on the tile surface as she retrieved the bag.

She placed it at the end of the bed, unzipped it, and flourished a pair of pajamas.

"Are those my NSYNC pajamas?"

"They are. Mama never forgets."

"That was probably more than ten years ago. I doubt if they fit." She closed her eyes and silently prayed. *Please don't fit.*

"You haven't grown that much since you were twelve. They were a little big to start with, too. I imagine they're perfect by now. I brought you some leggings, a shirt, and slippers. I didn't forget underwear, either."

"Thanks. I appreciate it." She hoped to stop her mother from pulling items out of the bag like a magician. Next thing would be the days-of-the-week panties. Her teen years were on display for the entire medical staff.

The nurse moved forward and accepted the pajamas. "I'll help her put them on after we take the x-rays. They'll be much nicer than the gown."

Oh yay. She had forgotten about the x-rays.

Chapter Fourteen

A FTER X-RAYS, SOME more probing, and another doctor who promised to give her the results but didn't, she ended up in a hospital room. Two attendants helped her onto the bed and hooked up her IV bag without exchanging a word with Nala.

"What's this?" She gestured to the room with gray walls and narrow windows with her hand with the IV catheter in it. Her left arm was in a sling to give her elbow a chance to recover.

One attendant shrugged, while the other wrinkled his nose and replied. "An awful decorating job. How can anyone expect to get better in these rooms? Would it kill them to put a live plant in here?"

Nala had to agree, but that wasn't her actual question. "The watercolor painting is decent. I meant, why am I in a hospital room?"

"You'll have to ask your doctor," the chatty attendant replied as they left, leaving the door open.

The last thing she needed was some enormous hospital bill on top of her replacement car expenses. Everyone knew emergency room visits were astronomical. Even though she carried her school insurance over, it wouldn't cover everything. If it was good for seventy-percent of the bill that would be wonderful, but it would still leave a hefty sum. There had to be someone she could talk to about this. After all, she didn't need to be here. She'd only got banged up some and lost her boot in the process. Max was the smarter one. He may have taken off before the explosion, but she wasn't sure. At least her dog was being looked after.

"Hello?" she called out when an employee pushing a cart went by.

No reply, which meant she hadn't timed her greeting right. There had to be a call button somewhere. A large plastic remote rested on her bed. The first button shot the end of her bed up at an awkward angle. Why anyone would want their feet stuck up like a mistreated action figure baffled her. The second button elevated her head and shoulders making her resemble those people who make their bodies into shapes for preschool videos. No time to be the letter V. She stabbed at the buttons with no results. It didn't make sense since they worked the first time. The third button with a person icon on it caused a buzzer to sound in the distance, or at least she thought it did. No one showed in what seemed like forever.

She had no cell phone or watch and no way to tell how much time had passed. She'd have to go find someone herself. If nothing else, she should at least have her cell phone, if the phone had survived the explosion. Her purse could be a casualty, too. The thought pulled a deep groan from her and heaviness settled on her already aching shoulders. Replacing her license would be a nightmare. No cell, no car, and who knows what else was missing.

The almost folded bed caused some issues, but she was able to wiggle out of it and stand, only her right hand was attached via tubing to an IV bag. Nala stared at the head of the needle that was pushed into her hand. Just looking at it made her queasy. No way she'd pull that out.

Instead, she reached for the bag that was hooked on a metal arm embedded in the wall. Her father was a big proponent of doing things yourself, except when he wasn't. The science fair fiasco served as an example. He wanted her project to be perfect. It ended with him doing everything and the teacher giving her a low grade because she didn't do it on her own. Her father even questioned the teacher about the winners since 'her' project was superior.

It was odd her parents weren't here to fuss over her. They might not even know where she was. By this time, her father would be in full work mode, trying to figure who would have the nerve to try to kill his daughter.

Kill was such a harsh word. Maybe it was a mistake. Her car's odometer had rolled over once already, possibly twice. It was possible Beetles self-destructed when they reached a certain age. More likely they just stopped, never to start again.

Nala got a grip on her IV bag and headed for the door, her bare feet making a slapping noise on the cold tile floor. A downward glance confirmed she did look as bad as she felt. Her right knee was bruised and swollen. The hairs stood out on her legs, reminding her she hadn't shaved them in almost forever. No need to in the winter, when normally everything would be covered up. Then, there was not having a boyfriend, too.

Oh well, it was what it was. She'd do good to find someone and resolve the mess. On the bright side, she didn't have on a drafty hospital gown. Too-tight boy-band shorty pajamas were far from her first choice, but it wasn't like she might run into someone she knew here.

A couple of hospital employees deep in conversation strolled by without even questioning her appearance in the hall. Good chance they were on break. A metallic squeak caused her to turn in time to spy another escaping patient. An elderly man leaned on his portable IV post while scouting out the area. He must have decided it was clear. He shuffled toward the elevator bank with the back of his robe flapping in the breeze.

Was she on the geriatric unit or the psych floor? All she wanted to do was go home, take a couple of aspirin, curl up in her own bed, and reflect on what happened.

She padded down the hall looking for someone in authority. Two of the smocked employees rushed over to the elevators to keep the old man from leaving. Maybe he'd had enough of being there, too.

After spending a good part of the day, and possibly the evening, being shuttled from place to place, the only thing she knew for sure was her elbow needed to rest, since pain radiated from there. The ability to relax would be so much easier in her own house. First, she had to get there. Uber was out. She hadn't a clue where her phone was. She didn't need the added expense anyhow. She'd call Karly. Her friend wouldn't make fun of her pajamas, even though she'd had a matching set when she was fourteen.

Since it didn't look like she'd get help of the authoritative type, she might as well help herself while people were busy escorting the resistant patient to his room. Nala had made it to the nurses' station, earning a few odd looks from visitors, but no direct inquiry. A panel inside the station showed an assortment of buttons which she assumed coordinated with the rooms. The majority of them were lit, which explained the lack of personnel at the station and why no one came when she buzzed.

Half-drunk cups of coffee sat on the desk, along with computer monitors and a landline phone. *Bingo!* All she'd have to do is call Karly. She stared at the console phone, wondering if she'd know how to use it. Not exactly the princess phone she had as a teen. Maybe there was a phone in her room. She hadn't checked. Well, she was here. She might as well try.

The wall around the station was a little higher than waist high, which made a simple reach over hard. If she went behind the wall, she'd surely be noticed. Still, what would happen to her? It wasn't as if she'd end up in jail for trying to use a phone. She sucked in her lips as she surveyed the area. Make it quick. *Act natural.* Two things that had got her into and out of tight spots before.

Although she could hear distant voices, no one was in sight. Nala pushed the gate wide to the nurses' station and strolled in as if she had the perfect right to be there, even though the sling and the fact she was holding her own IV bag shouted otherwise. She picked up the phone and held it to her ear. *Nothing.* No dial tone, which meant she had to push a number before she could call out or was she supposed to push a box on the phone to get a line to call out on? Confused, she gripped the receiver and stared at it. One of the boxes on the phone base was blinking. That meant someone was on hold. That much she remembered from working with her mother.

Nine was the number you normally needed to open an outside line. If there was still no dial tone, then she'd try one of those boxes for other lines. Her finger hovered over the nine.

"Nurse, I was wondering if you could…"

The voice froze her in place and not for the obvious reason of being caught doing something she shouldn't be doing. She recognized that voice and had hoped to never hear it again. *Escape, now.*

She placed the receiver back into the cradle and combed her hair with her right fingertips, causing the needle to pinch in her hand. Now all she had to do was subtly get past the man and not speak.

"Hey. What were you doing?"

She peered through her hair, and she kept her back straight, trying to retain as much dignity as possible while looking like a train wreck. *Attitude.* That's what she needed to get back to her room.

She managed to squeeze around the doctor while avoiding eye contact. He refused to move to make it easier for her, so she ended up brushing against him. As she headed back to her room, he followed. Fudge! Was anything going to be easy about this day? Better yet, would it ever end?

"It's obvious you're a patient here. I approve of your pajama choice. I used to date a girl who was into that band, too. She even listened to them after they broke up. I'd joked that they moved on. Maybe she should, too." He laughed out loud.

Nala groaned. It wasn't funny then, and it wasn't funny now. Besides, it wasn't like she was obsessed with the band. All she did was sing along when the songs came on the radio.

"I knew it was you!"

Great. Jeff, her former boyfriend and surgeon, was there on the exact same floor she was. What had she done to tick fate off? All she had to do was get to her room and jump in bed. Then she'd close her eyes and feign sleep. With any luck, someone would page the man. After all, he was supposed to be working. Eventually, he'd get tired of harassing her. No reason to spend much time on the old girl-friend, considering their relationship involved them both being in love with the same person—him.

She was almost back to her room. Ironic that the room she was trying to escape now served as a sanctuary. Her lack of response didn't stop Jeff from talking. "I knew you were up here. It's the whole reason I came up. Saw your mother downstairs. She managed to be gracious, but I could tell she wanted to stab me with the nearest scalpel. What did you tell her?"

Would he never leave? Her bed was still formed into a demented V, which would make it that much harder to climb into.

"Here, let me help you." Jeff moved forward, grabbed the remote and fixed the bed. "There you go."

She should thank him, but it would interfere with her not speaking to him. She managed to back up to the bed and hop onto it, then roll onto her back. She scooted under the covers, all under Jeff's watchful eyes. Finally, she broke. "Don't you have anything else to do?"

"This is much more fun." He reached for the IV bag. "Let me take that."

It would just be churlish to hold onto it. She handed him the bag as she tried to work her toes back under the blanket. If she had to see the man again, it'd always been her goal to look drop dead gorgeous, not like someone who had almost been blown up. He turned and saw what she was doing and pulled up the covers, tucking them around her.

"There you go. I'll stop back to see you soon."

As he turned to go, Tyler filled the door of the room.

Nala grumbled, "Don't bother."

The remark caused the handsome officer to take a step back.

"Not you," she corrected. "I meant him. Dr. Doofus."

Instead of acting offended, Jeff grinned. "She's trying to hide her true feelings."

Tyler glanced between the two of them. "Is there something going on I should know about?"

Besides her life taking a downward turn and gaining speed every second? "No, not really. How's Max?"

Chapter Fifteen

ORMALLY, TWO HANDSOME men fighting over her would be a fantasy. Nala exhaled, reminding herself they were far from fighting. If anything, Jeff showed up to gloat and to tell her about his perfect wife and super intelligent children. Odd he hadn't mentioned either. Instead of having the good taste to actually leave the room, he stood by the room door, smirking,

"Don't you have some lives to save?" Nala commented, hoping that it would remind the doctor he was on the clock.

"You're so right." Instead of ducking out of the door, he held out his hand to Tyler. "Jeff Winters, resident surgeon."

Tyler glanced at her as if asking for advice. Nala had none since she had no clue what game was being played.

"Tyler Goodnight, IPD." He took the outstretched hand and gave it a hard shake that had Jeff releasing the grip in a hurry.

"Please, I'm a surgeon," he managed to say, with the words sounding both offended and a little whiny. He threw a speculative glance in Nala's direction. "I should have guessed you preferred the brute strength type."

Before she could reply, the man whisked himself out the door, leaving Nala relieved, but Tyler continued to stare at where Jeff had been. "What was that about?"

Jeff's sudden reappearance in her life baffled her, too. He hadn't even taken the time to tell her how atrocious she looked. Before, he had been more the fashion police type than her own mother. Her hand went up to rub her neck, but the tug of the tubing stopped her before she could. Instead, she exhaled as she tried to come up with an excuse, but nothing clever or witty came to mind. "Wasted time, that's what Jeff was. I spent too much time thinking something might happen between us."

"Oh." His hand went up and scratched his cheek. "Can't see the two of you together. Was it serious?"

"Yes and no."

He shook his head. "That's no answer. That something the perps might say, when they're caught red-handed in the act of taking something that's not theirs while the store alarm is blaring. Come on, I expect better of you."

She closed her eyes ready to pretend fatigue, which wasn't a stretch at all. Still, no reason to make the same mistakes as before. When people don't know the truth, they imagine all sorts of things, usually never good. "I'm tired, my head hurts, and my car is history."

"Hey, I'm sorry." Tyler hurried to her side. His intention may have been to take her hand, but he settled for stroking her arm. "It was stupid of me to ask. Not my business. Forget about it."

He gave her an easy out she could have taken, but it was time to pull on her big girl panties and be clear about things. "We were in a relationship I thought was going somewhere, until it didn't."

"Okay." He gave her a sympathetic smile. "Appreciate the update. Any regrets?"

"Yes." The arm stroking stopped, which caused her to be clearer.

"I regret I didn't break up with the man sooner." What a fool she had been, always making excuses for his rude behavior. She felt she had to because he was a doctor, which somehow conferred on him the right to be obnoxious.

"I got news for you. He hasn't given up on you." His smile faded away as he said the words.

"Please." She wrinkled her nose at the absurdity. No way would Jeff be interested in her. She was so not the right type to be a talented surgeon's wife. "What makes you think that?"

"I walk in, and he's tucking you into bed. I'm fairly sure that's not the general procedure here. Then, what's up with his hand-shake?" Tyler's eyebrows went up in inquiry.

"He does like to say *surgeon* whenever introducing himself. He used to do that before he was even fully licensed, too, but never to anyone in the medical field who could look it up easily enough. He is very impressed with himself, and it never matters what anyone else thinks."

Tyler cleared his throat, but it may have been to cover a laugh. "I noticed that. I'm also willing to bet as long as you're in the hospital, you'll get another visit from dear old *please, I'm a surgeon*. You'd think I was trying to break his fingers."

"He's sensitive about his hands. They are magnificent tools." She rolled her eyes as she repeated the description Jeff so often used. "I have to get out of here before a repeat visit. How's Max?"

Tyler's heartbreaking grin made an appearance. "Outside of a few cuts from flying debris, he's great. The vet commented that often animals can sense disaster, usually the natural kind, but he may have leaped or run away before the explosion. Thankfully, he hung out in the general area."

She had wondered how the dog missed the general force of the blast. Since it all happened so fast, it was hard to say when Max took off. Maybe he even tried to get her away, but she dropped the leash when she dropped her purse. No reason to confess to accidently firing her weapon in a public place during that fiasco. The explosion, however, did do one positive thing.

"Where's my weapon? I think I must have dropped it at the park."

"I picked it up. After they loaded you up in the ambulance, I was walking to my car, but Max was determined to go back to the blast area. He found the gun, your purse, and your cell."

"Good dog."

"The way he hit on all your stuff immediately makes me wonder if he ever was a search and rescue dog or was in some type of police work. It was like he knew exactly what to do."

"Oh, no. He would have told me." Realizing her word fumble, she whimpered. "Head hurts."

"It must. It sounded like you said Max would have told you if he were a police dog before."

"Ha!" She forced a laugh. "Of course not. Police dogs are chipped just in case they get lost. They spend too much trouble and money training those dogs for them to end up in a shelter some-where. I appreciate your taking care of Max. Where is he now?"

"He's in my car. I wanted to bring him in, but the hospital can be funny about animals in the building." He shrugged his shoulders as if he couldn't figure out such behavior.

It was cold outside, and she didn't want Max to wait too long in the chilly temperatures. "My goal is to get out of the hospital today.

There really isn't anything wrong with me that I should be taking up a bed here."

Tyler opened his mouth to reply, but her mother's voice came out instead. "I agree," her mother announced as she strolled into the room. She flourished some papers in her hand. "I managed to spring you but only if someone is with you 24/7 because of the head injury. They wanted to keep you for observation, but I assured them as a trained nurse I could do whatever is necessary."

"You're not a nurse," Nala felt obliged to point out the obvious.

"Shhhh." Her mother held her finger up to her lips. "Do you want out of here or not?"

"Whatever you say, *Nurse* Gwen."

Her mother patted her blanket-shrouded legs. That's my girl." Gwen made a graceful swivel worthy of any runway model to address Tyler. "I'm sure you're here with a Max update."

"I am. He has a few cuts, but other than that, he's fine. He's waiting for me out in my car."

Gwen held up one finger. Even if Tyler was unaware, Nala recognized it as her general pose. "You bring Max over to our house in about forty-five minutes. That should give me enough time to get Nala released and drive her home. In fact, you can push her in the wheelchair while I go get the car."

Even though she caught the message she was going home with her parents to be fussed over, she *could* tolerate the current destination as long as she was leaving now. Once back at her childhood home, maybe she could convince someone to drive to her house under the guise of picking up clothes that weren't two sizes too small for her.

Tyler's warm baritone interrupted her planning. "I can do that. We need to be quick. We don't want Max to freeze," he added.

"All right, then, we need to get cracking." She clapped her hands together. "Where is that blue suitcase I brought?"

Nala decided this one time, because she was so tired, her mother could take charge. Heaven knows she was good at it.

Chapter Sixteen

AFTER TWO DAYS of her mother's loving ministrations, Nala's head no longer hurt, but she was fairly sure her nerves were shot. Here she was, installed in her childhood bedroom she felt had been preserved as a shrine. Her folks really should have had more children. It was a burden when you were the only one for the parents to pin their expectations on.

After her mother had driven her to the doctor for a check-up, which resulted in her being told to take it easy and continue to wear her sling, Gwen served Nala ants on a log. Not actual ants on a log, but celery stuffed with peanut butter and dotted with raisins. It was a snack Nala had learned to make in Daisy Scouts. Even though the snack was tasty, it made her feel like she *was* back in Daisy Scouts. She did the only thing she could do—picked up her pink princess phone and begged Karly to come over and hopefully break her out.

The numbers on the clock radio barely moved. Was this one of those time warp things where everything stopped? Max, who was supposed to be her friend, deserted her as soon as her mother headed to the kitchen. Apparently, food triumphed over everything. Not a reassuring thought with robbers often bringing drugged meat to get around family pets. At least she had nothing to steal or so she thought. A robber wouldn't know until he or she broke in. With no one at her house, it could be a prime target.

She stretched her right hand. It was still sore and bruised from the IV, but usable, and there was no real reason she couldn't be at home. The lack of transportation could be problematic, but she'd work that out. Fortunately, her father had picked up her laptop at the office and all the insurance work Sawyer left behind. It had given her something to do, but she had finished it. Karly could help her with the Dog Park Romeo case, which was all she had going, since she hadn't heard from Elvin or Tyler, which made her suspect her mother was running interference on the phone. It wasn't unusual for the phone to ring once, then, not again.

Sometimes, her mother would declare it was the wrong number, and other times she pretended the phone hadn't rung at all. Even though Tyler had retrieved her cell for her, it no longer worked. Being hurtled through the air and slammed down on hard surface tended to do that to phones. The new model should be here anytime. The doorbell rang, and she hoped it was either the new phone or Karly. She lowered the volume on the television to listen.

"You go on up. I'll make you girls some snacks," her mother chirped.

"Thank you, Mrs. Bonne."

The sound of steps running up the stairs preceded Karly bursting through the door. Her flushed face alarmed Nala.

"What's wrong?"

Karly collapsed on the bed and gasped. "You have no idea how hard it is running up the stairs holding your breath."

"Why would you? It wasn't like we had made a dare. Remember that game we used to play when we were younger? Truth or Dare." Her friend's behavior struck her as strange, but then everything did after *the incident,* as she'd decided to call it. Somehow, calling it the incident made it less frightening and turned it into something annoying or embarrassing such as wearing two different shoes to work. Her brain took a hard rattle, which might be why it felt like everything was a little off-kilter.

"That game was never much fun without boys. There were never any great dares such as licking someone's cheek or biting their earlobe."

Licking? She wrinkled her nose. "You spend way too much time around dogs."

"I do," Karly agreed with a grin and stretched out on the bed, kicking her shoes off. "Besides, I was trying not to laugh when your mother greeted me and told me to go upstairs. It felt like a flashback."

"Welcome to my world." Nala gestured to the posters and the pink gingham drapes.

"Why didn't you ever change anything? You know your mother was probably itching to make the room over."

Why hadn't she? It bore some thought. Nala had spent her last year of high school working hard to keep her grades up and continued on with all the extra training, so her father could make her a stellar candidate for the police academy. It hadn't come to the point where she had decided against the academy. She even took a few law enforcement classes in college, which became electives when she switched majors. All her design efforts went into her dorm room. "I just kept thinking I would leave. Why bother?"

"For times like these, I guess." Karly stared up at the ceiling where a poster of a young male actor was situated over the bed. "Your parents were okay with that?" She pointed upward. "My dad would have freaked."

"Yeah, he would have."

In Karly's big noisy family, her father had some absolute rules. The only person allowed to work their way around the rules was his wife. Nala lowered her voice to a gruff timber to imitate Karly's father.

"No long-haired hippie guy will be hanging over his girl's bed. Poster or not."

"Spot on. What's the deal with your father? I expected him to be extra protective."

Nala stretched out on her back beside her friend to stare up at the poster. "He does have nice eyes. Every night I'd look up at him and tell him goodnight. As for my room, my father stopped coming in about the time I got my first bra. I think he thought he was giving me my privacy, but it was more likely he was afraid of finding bras or tampons everywhere. Or worse, an open diary that he would have to refrain from reading."

Karly pushed on one elbow and pantomimed as if opening a book. "Tuesday, October fifth. Dear Diary, we had a math test that I naturally aced. I let that cute boy that just moved in see my answers."

"I swear you never forget anything. See if I ever tell you anything juicy. Also, I need you to drive me to my house. I would prefer to have current clothes as opposed to those I left behind. Any other mother would have thrown them out or taken them to Goodwill."

Her bedroom door opened without a knock. Her mother balanced a tray of goodies on one hip with one hand and entered the room. "What's this about Goodwill?"

Before anyone could reply, Gwen shot Nala a censorious look.

"No daughter of mine will be wearing thrift shop finds."

"Mrs. Bonne," Karly interrupted, "They have some good stuff there. I've picked up designer clothes, even ones with tags still on them."

Her mother looked unconvinced and set the tray on the dresser. There was the pad of dog paws on the stairs, which meant Max had given up his stay in the kitchen. "I got you girls your favorites, Dr. Pepper and Fritos." She turned to go as Max pushed into the room, but pivoted back on the heel of her classic pumps. "Sweetie, if you need clothes, you're welcome to borrow some of mine since we're the same size."

"Thanks, Mom." She forced a smile while contemplating how she would *not* be wearing her mother's clothes. The door clicked shut as Karly worked herself into a sitting position.

"Wow, I could wear my mother's clothes." She gestured to a current T-shirt, which featured a movie long since forgotten by most. "Instead of looking like someone who's unwilling to let go of the past, I'll look like I ran smack into fifty plus fashion."

"A very elegant fifty. Don't let your mother hear you say that. She's convinced everyone that she's forty. My mother did the math and is shocked that your father would marry a child."

"Ha. Ha." It was a standing joke with her mother that she had been a child bride.

Karly strolled over to the dresser and picked up a sweating glass of soda and a handful of corn chips. "You want anything?"

"A car."

Karly glanced back at the tray. "I don't see one. We do need to get you one."

"I'd like some chips," Max pointed his nose up in the direction of the food.

Karly put her handful on the floor, then got more. "Your mother is the only person I know who actually puts corn chips in a glass bowl. We also have cloth napkins. Fancy."

"I'm tired of Chez Bonne. The reason my parents treat me like I'm still fifteen is that I've never grown up in their eyes. For Pete's sake, Dr. Pepper and corn chips. I liked that as a kid."

Karly chewed noisily, then swallowed. "I still do. What are you eating now? Finger sandwiches?"

"Usually whatever is on sale at the market. Most of the time, it's popcorn or hummus and bagel chips, often with a diet soda." She sighed. "It's not my parents. They're just trying to take care of me. My mother even took time off from work, and you know what a control freak she is, so that was major. What's really bothering me is all my work just ground to a halt."

She hesitated, cleared her throat, and added, "Now, the incident. Sure, I hadn't gotten a lead on my Dog Park Romeo, but I *was* trying. Tyler and I had gotten to the point where we were talking about seeing each other again. The only one thing I wanted was for my parents not to know. I can just see my mother doing something awful such as inviting Tyler to Sunday dinner and asking how many children he wanted."

"That would be a little over the top, even for her." Karly sipped her drink, but paused to ask, "What's up with you and Tyler?"

"My goal was to date discreetly. My father listened to the surveillance tape from Max's collar for a clue on who planted the bomb. I'm sure he heard our plans to date under the radar."

"He said nothing?"

"Not a peep. I can't expect to date while living here. I don't even have my replacement phone so it isn't like Tyler could call me."

"True." Karly crunched another chip. "You have his number?"

"In my broken phone. You, my parents, and my own number are the only ones I memorized. That's not going to work. I'll have to stay here until my new phone arrives, which could be today or tomorrow. I thought we could brainstorm about Dog Park Romeo."

She scooted to the edge of her bed and picked up a paper tablet and pen. "I'm grateful it's my left hand that's in a sling, although driving a stick will be challenging with my hurt knee and bruised hand."

"Automatic is what you need and something with a little more power than two hamsters running an exercise wheel. You have to be able to follow folks and get away from them, too. Six cylinders, at least."

"Yeah." Still, it was hard to get over losing Natalie, her car. She felt like the car defined who she was. If she were honest with herself, she was never the hippie or hipster type. As a private investigator, she needed a low-profile car—something there were a lot of and nothing too flashy. "I've needed a new car forever, but I didn't want to spend the money. Any thought on the dog park guy?"

"Well, I don't think he's been back at Broad Ripple. Maybe he's moved on." Karly retrieved the chip bowl and offered it to Nala. "There are tons of dog parks now."

"Tons?" Nala had been on the lookout for dog parks, but she seriously doubted there were *tons*. As long-time friends, she knew Karly enjoyed exaggerating. "Such as?"

"I know there's one in Clay Terrace. You can shop and take your dog for a walk. There's several in Indy including Waggin' Tails Bark Park, Smock Bark Park, and Living the Dog Life. I think there may be a dozen or more. Maybe not a ton. Just a figure of speech."

Nala bit into a chip, enjoying the salt and rough texture. Now she remembered why she liked them before she became so concerned about calories. "Hmmm, more than I thought. It will take a while to check all those out. Maybe we should come from a different angle. If it's one dude, then he has multiple dogs. I'm sure this is possible."

Max placed his head on the bed. "Do you think he might be changing dogs to confuse people?"

"I did think that," Nala remarked.

"And," Karly held up her hand, "dog lovers would remember the dog, not the person."

"Some," Nala agreed. "Those who were actually going out with the man remembered him. Young Mark Harmon. I'm wondering if the man owns the dogs or is borrowing them. If he's borrowing them, it's possible he's a new member at the dog park. Neither woman mentioned anything about the dogs not being well behaved. If someone borrowed a dog, they might not behave for that person. What do you think?"

Max lifted up his head. "I think anyone who uses dogs to trick dog lovers out of money should be locked up."

"My feelings exactly," Nala said, but Max wasn't done talking.

"Cheeseburgers. Think of all the cheeseburgers that the money could have bought."

Nala closed her eyes. Should have known. It came down to cheeseburgers with Max. Too often, she expected her dog to think like a person. "Karly, can you help me?"

"I did call around the shelters, and there haven't been too many overnighters or weekenders. At least, none matching your description. We have folks who decide to adopt a pup, then they discover how much attention is necessary, then back comes the dog. I do have an idea where our boy might be getting his dogs from, though."

"Do tell." It was more than she had so far.

"Dog walker. A dog walker shows up at dog parks. He could even do reconnaissance work. Find out which parks have the most prospects. Quite a few business people work long hours and use the dog walkers to take care of their pet. Some of them spend more time with the dog than the actual owner does. I wouldn't be surprised if a dog acted better for the walker than its owner. It all kinda fits."

Chapter Seventeen

EVEN THOUGH KARLY and Nala tiptoed down the carpeted stairs to avoid the inevitable questions about where they were going, Max didn't. He galloped down the stairs possibly even more excited about going home than Nala and barked when he hit the foyer. Nala held her breath. It would be hard to miss hearing the full-throated bark. Her mother would fuss over her and imply she wasn't well enough to go anywhere.

The incident may have shaken her up, but no one was giving her paid sick days, which meant she needed to get back to work. Her first priority would be to have age appropriate clothes. Another one would be the ability to work uninterrupted. Her mother kept checking on her, possibly to see if she had fallen into a coma. She glanced toward the kitchen door. No movement there. Maybe her mother hadn't heard. As hard as it was to believe, it looked like she was in the clear. Nala released the breath she was holding.

"I'm glad you girls came downstairs. It saves me a trip," her mother announced, startling Nala in the process. Karly leaned up against the wall and mouthed something incomprehensible.

"Uh, yeah, we did."

Her mother wore her bronze trench coat and had set it off with a dark fedora with a feathered hatband. Sugar cookies! Her mother was dressed in classic private investigator garb, looking fabulous. What if her mother insisted, she needed to help Nala out due to the incident? It didn't bear thinking about. She scrunched up her face as if she tasted something bitter.

"Stop that," her mother declared. "Such expressions cause wrinkles. You certainly don't want your face to be puckered in such a manner. People will be forever asking what's wrong with you for the rest of your life. Anyhow, I have to go."

A horn sounded outside. Gwen gestured to the door with her driving gloves gripped firmly in one hand. "That's your father." She placed her empty hand on Nala's cheek. "You're going to be excited."

"About what?" She knew from years of living with her mother, whatever Gwen Bonne found exciting, she did not. When she was six, she may have liked matching dresses, but not when she was twenty.

Her mother chuckled. "Oh no, you're not getting it out of me. It will be mutually beneficial." She strolled away with a sly smile and slammed the door behind her.

"Hmm," Karly mused, "what could be mutually beneficial to both of you?"

"I'm afraid my mother is off to buy herself a grandchild. I'm just surprised Dad is helping her."

"Yeah, like that would happen. We might as well get going while the coast is clear."

Even though she heard her friend, she was concentrating on what her mother could be up to. With her mother, it was best to stay one step ahead to avoid getting steamrolled. "She had driving gloves in her hands."

"Those were driving gloves. I've heard of them, but I've never seen anyone actually wear them while driving." Karly fished the car keys out of her hoodie pocket, then headed to the front door. "Your mother wears them?"

"Not all the time and definitely not in the summer. They are more like something she puts on to impress people, like she's a professional driver or something." Her shoulders went up in a shrug. Her mother was all about appearances, which fit in with her design business. Half the time, she had no clue who her mother was trying to impress.

"Sounds like you have a family mystery there. I'll start the stopwatch on my phone, and we can see how long it will take you to crack the case."

"It sounds like a losing bet to me." No one understood why her mother did things, including her father, and he'd had years to figure the woman out. She followed Karly, waited for Max to shoot through the opening before locking the door. What's happening with you and Harry?"

Karly pivoted fast enough to give herself whiplash. "You said something to him, didn't you?"

Well aware her friend would be upset at her very minor interference, she deflected the question with one of her own. "Why?"

"He called up and asked what the hours of the shelter were, which was weird because the hours are posted on the website. I can't believe I forgot to mention it to you"

They strolled across the curving front walk to Karly's car parked in the driveway. Her friend had no clue what a concession it was for her mother to allow her friend to use the front drive. Whenever her father drove home in a squad car, he had to park in the back or in the garage. She didn't want the neighbors to think they were in trouble. Max veered off as he headed toward a bush that just managed to hold onto its waxy green leaves. "No! Get in the car!"

"Spoilsport," her dog grumbled as he sauntered past and whacked Nala with his tail.

Once the three of them were in the car and her mother's bushes were free from Max's watering efforts, she could turn her attention back to Harry. "Did he say anything about adopting a pet?"

"No, but I assumed he was. Why else would he want to know the hours?"

Could her friend be that dense? Her eyes rolled upward for a brief second, then she said, "To see you."

The car purred to life, and Karly reversed out of the long drive. Personally, Nala didn't mind parking in the back. It meant minimal backing up.

"Did you even consider that?"

Karly's shoulders slumped a little. "I did. It would make no sense because I treated the man horribly. There's no reason for him to get a dog."

Revealing her conversation with Harry was tempting. Before she could, Max rested his large head on Karly's shoulder. "People go to the shelter to get pets."

Sometimes, it takes a dog to say the obvious. Only this dog continued speaking.

"They are incredibly lonely and often have trouble relating with other humans. They need companionship. Let's face it, a cat won't do it. Cats expect to be worshipped. Isn't that kinda like your old boyfriend?" He turned his head slightly to direct the question to Nala.

Okay, maybe she had been lonely and taken to talking to herself, but she'd read Einstein did it, too. Didn't he have trouble relating to other people? She pursed her lips as she tried to remember what she'd read a number of years ago in the book on the man. It didn't matter. "Karly, I'm not sure I will forgive you for sharing my love life with Max even before I met him."

Her friend chuckled. "Geesh, I'm sorry. You have to admit he nailed it with Jeff. I bet he expected you to worship at his feet. That's why he showed up on your hospital floor to give you one more chance."

"Not hardly." She gave a derisive snort. Age and Jeff had done a number on her. She wouldn't fall for his line of bull again. "Besides, he's probably married by now. A doctor is still a catch no matter how obnoxious he is. Some women might even like being ordered around."

"I don't know any."

"Me, either. Do you have Elvin's number in your phone?" It was past time she heard from the man, but he was probably stymied, too, by her not having a phone.

"Yes. Before you ask, I also have Tyler Goodnight's number."

Most women wouldn't turn their nose up at the handsome officer, but her friend? There were unwritten rules with besties. You didn't date your bestie's exes, current squeeze, or even lifetime crushes. The look she shot her friend must have been easy to decipher.

"Come on. You know me better than that. Besides, I'm still hung up on Harry, somewhat. Tyler contacted me to find out more about you. By the way, this is top secret, you're not to say a word about it. He wanted me to call him if you ever needed help or were in trouble."

In that aspect, the man reminded her of her father. "He did, huh?"

"Personally, I think it's sweet," Karly added with a smirk. "I know you can take care of yourself, but he wants to help because he cares, and I'm betting the spark is still there."

"It is," she admitted. "Still, that's something sneaky my father might do."

"Oh yeah. Since I'm spilling my secrets, I have your father on speed dial, too."

"Karly!" She didn't even know her friend anymore. "Did he also ask you to call if his little princess got into something too difficult to handle?"

"Your dad never talks like that. One day, he came into the shelter and told me to put his number on speed dial, because if I or you needed help, he could get things done. Let's face it, my pop can't get things done unless you need someone to grill a burger to perfection."

"Speaking of burgers…" Max started.

"No!" Both women said together, then laughed. Nala decided to soften the blow. "Maybe later." She turned to face Karly, who still had a dog head on her shoulder. "Max, get back. You could cause an accident. I'm calling Elvin, then Tyler. He might not pick up if he's at work." She suited her actions to her words and waited for the phone to ring and placed it on speaker, so she wouldn't have to repeat everything once she hung up.

"Hello, and thank you for calling the Starry Skies Mental Hospital. If you need to reach a patient, please press one and then say their name."

"Elvin!" Why did the man always have to mess with her? The short answer was it was who he was.

"You didn't press one."

She sighed, pressed one, but didn't expect anything to happen.

"That patient has been denied phone privileges. He has run up the hospital phone bill calling 900 numbers."

"I'm sure Amy would like to hear about that."

"Nala. Don't. It was a joke. You have to be the most humorless person I know."

She sighed. It wasn't the first time Elvin complained about her lack of humor. Sometimes she wondered. Was it her? She glanced over at Karly who shook her head. It had to be Elvin just wasn't as funny as he thought he was. Could it be other guys found him amusing? Considering how much he was bullied in high school, that would be a no.

"I'll laugh when you're funny, not before. Find anything on the dog collar or the pin?"

"The pin was destroyed by the explosion. If you didn't see anyone attaching a bomb to your car, the pin didn't, either. As for Max's collar, I heard you and Officer Goodnight making plans to get back together, and you flirting with another guy, too. You're such a Jezebel."

"I wasn't flirting. It was work."

"That's what I tell Amy, too."

"You're a professional hacker, snoop, security expert, whatever your official title is. When do you actually talk to flesh and blood people?"

"I'm talking to you. I spoke with your father when I gave him a copy of the tape."

"Lemon bars! I wanted to keep any possible relationship with Tyler on the QT."

"Yeah, I heard that on the tape along with a reference about your father going overboard."

She lifted her hand to the back of her head. "The pounding is back. My skull feels like it's about to crack open. Did you find out anything else about Magnus?"

"It pains me to say this, but no. Maybe the witness protection story is true. Someone was busy erasing electronic footprints. I even went back to where I was before and that information is now gone. On the flip side, he could be super dirty and has folks more talented than me wiping everything."

The witness protection story was too easy. Besides, what person who is told to stay low, walks into a cop bar to meet a girl? It could happen, but so far none of her cases had been simple or easy. "Let's say it is the latter. Could you give me the names of these people? Your competitors in the area?"

"I could give you some, but keep in mind they aren't necessarily around the corner. Those who dabble in dark work usually are in other countries. Ones they can't be extradited from. They also don't have names like John Hogan or Felicia Adams. It's Felix the Fox, Red Run, and one is a series of numbers. Some you have to contact inside of online video games. It's not like I can give you a name and you just pop over and ask a few questions."

"I have faith in you. Put your ear to the ground and see if you hear anything."

"The Bonne family is going to be the death of me."

The family? She knew she wouldn't like the answer, but she had to ask. "What do you mean?"

"Your father was here with an entire list of people. He wanted to know if they were somehow making contact from behind bars. He wanted *anything* since it could be in code. Oh, and he wants it yesterday. Then, your mother comes by with actual money and pays me in advance to investigate—wait for it—Tyler Goodnight."

Nala squeezed her eyes shut. "Say it isn't so."

"It is. I know your mother is expecting some dirt, but so far, nothing. The guy is clean. He got in a fight while serving abroad with a civilian, but sometimes those things are inevitable when in uniform. No charges were pressed on either man. He's not married, which is what your mother really wanted to know, and currently has no children."

"I don't know what to say."

"You can say thank you. Also, thank your mother. She saved you a lot of work investigating the man. Of course, you wouldn't have because that would be wrong if you're dating."

Even though Karly wasn't part of the call, it didn't stop her from chirping in. "Come on. Nala has the tools to investigate. When you start dating someone is the perfect time to peek into the closets, so you don't get a big surprise later."

Elvin picked up on little things. He should have been her partner as opposed to Sawyer, but to do the work he did, it was always best if he were unknown. Nala knew her friend would have a clever name he used for hacking. "Hey, what's your hacker name?"

"If I told you, I'd have to kill you afterwards."

"Ha! Ha! Very funny."

"I wasn't kidding. Out." The phone clicked, signaling he'd hung up.

"Sometimes," Nala began. "I don't know what to think about Elvin."

"He's a character." Karly announced with an eyeroll.

"Yeah," Nala agreed, then wrinkled her nose. "I hate to admit it, but he was right about investigating Tyler. I would never have done it. Consider it a breach of trust. How can you have a relationship if you don't trust one another?"

Chapter Eighteen

A SENSE OF normalcy settled over Nala as she entered her home. Max charged ahead, barking and inspecting each room. On the positive side, he didn't chase out any robbers or squatters. Similar to her dog, she checked each room, but instead of inspecting for intruders, she was familiarizing herself with what made up her home.

Her unmade bed represented a relaxed attitude her mother didn't enjoy. The only time Nala had ever been allowed to leave her bed unmade was if she was in it. Her mother had some pithy saying about if you made the bed up first, cleaning the rest of the room would go faster. A book still rested on her bedside table. Hard to believe she'd only been gone two days. It felt as if she were returning after a long trip.

Karly called from the kitchen. "You have no decent snacks!"

"I know. The incident interrupted my grocery run. It's on my list of things to do." She ambled down the hall into the kitchen.

Her friend peered into the fridge while Max watched her. Karly withdrew two cans of diet soda and handed one to Nala. As she closed the fridge door with her hip, she commented, "You have a bachelor fridge. Plenty of condiments, but no real food. Instead of beer, you have diet soda. Didn't your mother teach you better?"

At any time of the year, her mother had enough food to withstand a six weeks siege. She dated the cans and frozen goods to use them in a timely fashion. "You know she did. I don't want to go to that much work, and besides, food isn't cheap. One extended electrical outage and I'd lose everything."

"Yeah, that's me, too, not buying food because of a possible electrical outage in the near future."

She knew her friend was teasing.

"Why don't you try to call the dog walking places using your official capacity? Tell them you want to recommend their services. Then, ask about the guy. I'll get something to wear that is age appropriate and load up on my toiletries, so I don't smell like gardenias. That must be the required old lady scent. There's also camelias, too."

Karly glanced up from her phone. "Don't forget lily of the valley."

"All white flowers," Nala mused to herself.

The secret to getting work done was to get back into her office. She needed to send back the results using Sawyer's computer. She could use her own, but any future work would come via Sawyer's email. Who knows? The man himself might contact her through his email. It might be weird, but everyone knew their own email. Besides, he left it open so she could do just that. It wasn't like she'd be snooping.

Once she located a suitcase in the back of the closet in the second bedroom, she threw clothes, shoes, her book, and toiletries into it. She didn't want to pack too much because not having enough gave her an excellent reason to return back to her home.

Her father insisted she carried comprehensive coverage on her car. The agent explained it covered items not associated with driving such as a tree limb shattering her windshield or her garage collapsing on her car. Surely an explosion would be covered. Whatever she got might not be much, but it could be a down payment. "Wait! I just got an idea."

Max nudged her and asked the inevitable question. "Cheeseburger?"

"No, not yet." She thought about telling the vet to tell her to cut out cheeseburgers for her canine, but that would never work. Besides, she'd just feel guilty. Until now, Max had had a hard life. It wouldn't hurt him to put on a few pounds. "Karly, any luck with the dog walkers?"

"Not really. I called the first service, Tail Waggers. When I asked for a specific walker, they wanted a name, which I didn't have. I told the receptionist that he looked like that guy on that naval cop show with the initials, but younger. She told me she didn't watch television. Can you believe that? A person who doesn't watch television? It's unamerican."

"I doubt it's unamerican. You can give them both names: Allan and Edward. That might net us someone. Still, they are common names, which was probably the point. Maybe you can ask if there's a specific park the walkers use. My gut instinct is our guy is going where the money is, which means we need parks in the high end of town. I doubt he's driving his client's dog across town." She scowled at the wall. Here she was going off half-cocked about dog walkers, which Romeo might *not* be. It was the thinnest of leads, but hanging out at the dog park wasn't helping.

A knock sounded on the door. *Odd.* She wasn't expecting anyone. Curious neighbors might have seen a different car in the drive and decided to check it out. Most folks would say they were looking out for her, when in actuality, they were just nosy. Since it was her house it made sense that she answered the door. The open curtains allowed her to see the front of a squad car.

As she swung open the door, expecting to see a certain officer, she wasn't disappointed. Officer Goodnight stood there looking sheepish. "What are you doing here?" she asked.

"My job. Every couple of hours someone drives by the house just to make sure things are okay. I was on the loop and saw Karly's car." He nodded in the direction of the station wagon covered with rescue dog stickers.

"How did you know it was Karly's car?"

"Wild guess." The corners of his lips twitched the tiniest bit as he tried to fight a smile. "I called in the numbers to be safe. If Karly was in the vicinity, I figured you would be, too."

Not wanting to share a conversation that could turn personal, she opened the screen door to join Tyler on the porch. It must have looked like an invitation because Max barreled through the opening and greeted Tyler with a series of yips.

The officer squatted and ruffled the thick hair around Max's neck. "To answer your question, I didn't bring you a snack. If I'd known you were here, I would have."

A whimper sounded as Max eased into a prone position with his head on his paws, his classic pose when he didn't get what he wanted.

"Look at him," Tyler stood and gestured to the canine who refused to look back at him.

"No need to," Nala said.

Despite her words, she found herself observing her pooch. The act was an old one, which was probably the reason it didn't have the same impact on her. "I've watched the same act enough. Dogs can be like little kids. They have tantrums, too."

"Yeah. I heard something like that from the canine handlers. I would have sworn that Max understood me when I told him I didn't bring him anything." The furrowed brows announced his concern.

No matter what Nala could say, she'd probably just come off sounding mean with her theatrical dog. He should be in movies. Her only option was to change the subject. "Karly drove me over here to get some clothes."

"I figured as much. I could have driven you, too."

"It would have been awkward with my parents, you know."

He gave a short nod. "I don't think we're fooling them. Your father made a point of telling me you didn't have a working cell if I'd tried to call."

"Did you?"

"I did. Left a voice mail. I just wanted to know how you were doing."

A warm feeling unfolded deep in her center. It must have been how Rudolph the reindeer felt when he discovered his secret crush liked him and suddenly that he could fly. Okay, maybe she couldn't fly, but he *did* care. While she assumed, he cared, it wasn't the same as hearing him say it. "I think I'll have a phone tomorrow, then I can move back."

"That would be a mistake. Have you even talked to your father?" His voice rose in volume and intensity. He shifted his weight from one foot to the other. "It was definitely a bomb. Torres, who's on the squad, told me it was a sophisticated piece of work. None of the pipe bomb stuff that high school kids might make. That should scare you. It scares me." His superior height allowed him to glance down at her while the bill of his hat shadowed his face.

Some might find the pose intimidating, but she refused to and crossed her arms. "I'm not a little girl. I can take care of myself."

"The answer is no, then?"

"Maybe." She shook her head, not wanting to argue. "Never mind. My parents took off before we left. There was no one to tell. It would be even better if I could work at the office without my mother popping in every fifteen minutes to check on me."

He eased an arm around her shoulders. "I know you have a job to do, but you need to be careful. There's someone out there who wants to hurt you. Would it kill you to be a little more cautious?"

"If the alternative is murder, I guess I could take things slower." From the corner of her eye, she saw an unfamiliar, new car turn onto her street. It raced down the street too fast. "This doesn't look good."

"Take cover!" Tyler yelled, withdrew his arm from around her shoulder, pulled his weapon, and took a defensive stance behind a porch column.

The spritely *beep-beep* of a car horn had her groaning from her place on the cold cement.

Chapter Nineteen

TYLER, WHO WAS half-hidden from view by the porch pillar, confirmed Nala's suspicions. "Stand down. It's your mother and father in a new car."

There was a slight crunch as the tires of the car rolled across the hardened skiff of snow in her driveway. It did explain why her mother needed her driving gloves. Nala pushed up from the cement slowly. Max, who had adopted a similar position, lurched into action, barking, ready to greet the two.

Nala winced, envisioning long scratches on the car door. "Don't jump on the car."

Most of the time Max didn't jump on cars, but there was always that odd time. Her mother kept her cars pristine. They were detailed every six months even if they didn't need it, and they never did. The trade-in value was always great with the excellent condition and low mileage. Whenever her parents drove anywhere, her father drove his car, which was more of a performance vehicle than her mother's roomy sedans that shouted *grandmother* or *real estate agent.*

The fact her mother was test driving cars must mean her current car had reached the three-year mark or had lost the new car smell.

Tyler holstered his weapon and smiled at Nala. "I guess we should check out the new ride."

"Yeah," Nala agreed. However, from her position, it looked a lot like the old ride only it had a paper sale sticker on the window. Her mother preferred dark cars because they were classic and referred to light-colored cars as *common,* as if cars had a caste system. There were tons of white cars in the area which would earn the undesirable label. The electronic windows went down as they moved closer.

Her father nodded at Tyler. "Good to see you were on the job and took appropriate action. I'm impressed that you got Max to take cover, too."

"Part of my job, sir."

Nala noticed that he made no mention that Max took cover on his own. Her dog, if he was nothing else, was a survivor. She waved at her parents. "New wheels, huh?"

Her mother beamed. "I think this one is the winner. We were waiting for the price to go down in December, but then they didn't have the model I wanted. Todd, our sales guy, was able to locate the model and have it shipped here. The holidays slowed things down, but he promised us the December price."

It sounded like a done deal. "What's different about this car than the previous one?"

The cars looked about the same, but every car couldn't be an iconic vehicle, like her recently departed car. Her eyes scanned the vehicle for some type of ornamentation that would identify the brand. Had her mother ordered the same model?

"It has all these new controls on the steering wheel—" her mother started.

Her father interrupted her. "Which she knows nothing about." He earned a poke from his wife for his remark as she picked up where she had left off.

"There are tons of safety features, too. It has seat warmers and seat coolers. The seats are luxurious and have lumbar support for long drives."

"Mother, you never drive anywhere that far away."

"True," her mother acknowledged. "If I did, I would have the lower back support I need. And, best of all," she announced with a wide grin and leaned over her husband as much as she could to address her daughter. "You can have my old car."

Even though she heard the words, Nala mentally retraced her mother's exit from the house. Her father drove, which in itself wasn't that unusual, but he drove his car. No way would he trade in his baby. "Ah, Mother, don't you need it as a trade-in?"

Her mother lifted her nose up and gave a dismissive sniff. "Do you think I'm poor? My business hasn't run its course, yet."

"No, I didn't say that." She stifled the urge to sigh, which her mother would view as an insult. Recently, her mother had been commenting on how much better her bottom line was, once they removed the embezzler from their midst.

"Besides, I want to help you out."

A vehicle would be nice. With her arm in a sling, a sedan with power steering would be a lot easier than rack and pinion, which sometimes she had to strong-arm around tight corners. "I was planning on getting my own vehicle. I need to contact my insurance company."

Her mother's happy expression melted away while her father added, "Can't you let your mother do something nice for you as opposed to being so damn independent? You're our only child. We don't have anyone else to fuss over."

Even though her father's stern expression didn't even hint at grandchild, Nala thought she could hear an underlying message. If she would kindly provide them with grandchildren, they wouldn't hover over her so much. "I need to find out the insurance payoff."

"I called already. They would only give you a thousand for your totaled vehicle. We both know that will get you a really nice scooter. It would be hard to balance Max on the back."

Her father had a point. Even though she hadn't warmed up to the idea of a different vehicle, she had hoped to do it on her own. Her previous car had been a much-loved gift, but she never had the chance to car shop on her own. "I wouldn't mind borrowing it until I get another vehicle. What about Max and the upholstery?"

Sensing a victory in the offing, her mother's smile returned. "I ordered some special seat covers. It will preserve the value of the car. It would also help if you didn't eat in it."

It would only be for a little while, she reminded herself. All she had to do was get the insurance payout and money owed to her for completing Sawyer's cases, and it should be enough for a down payment.

Tyler, who stood right behind her, spoke in a low voice. "It would be an excellent undercover vehicle."

For a *grandmother*, she added in her head. Wasn't that the idea? No one she was tailing would be suspicious of such a car. "Thanks, Mother."

Oh, they thought they had won. Her parents turned to stare at each other and shared a knowing look. A shared look could contain an entire conversation. More than the car, she wished she had someone to exchange gazes with like her parents did. Even though she tried not to do it, she pivoted in an effort to peek at Tyler. He raised his eyebrows as if asking what she wanted to know. Maybe they might develop a silent communication. Only time would tell.

★

A HEAVY PACKING quilt covered the leather seats of Nala's newest ride as she eased down the road, driving with one hand. The large form of her standing dog made it almost impossible to see out the right window. "Max, sit down."

He plopped his rump down, but not without comment. "You don't have to be a grump about it. Roomy new cars make me happy."

"Of course, they do. You don't realize the strings that go along with such a gift?"

"Strings?" He tilted his head. "I don't see any? Could be some on the rug I'm sitting on."

"It's a quilt. Besides, the strings are more for me than you. They think I can't make it on my own and have to help me out."

"They didn't say that. I would have heard. I have excellent hearing."

"For some things," Nala spoke the words in a sotto voice.

"I heard that!"

"Figured you would." She shook her head. It would be hopeless getting a canine to understand human family dynamics. "Next thing my mother will be wanting to do is help me with the Dog Park Romeo case—again."

"Might as well. You're not getting anywhere with it."

Nala glared at her dog. The music, which had been playing low, cut out as her phone rang. No matter the strings, it was handy to have a phone she could answer using her steering wheel. It was a number she knew.

"Hello, Elvin. What's up?"

"Nothing. That's the problem."

"How so?" She really wasn't following the conversation. All she knew was that her friend and subcontractor wasn't his usual wise-cracking self.

"As you know, your mother had me investigate your newest squeeze, Tyler Goodnight."

"He's not my squeeze." She felt the need to protest since they were only at the talking stage.

"Whatever," he uttered the word, then continued. "Didn't find any dirt on the man. Lo and behold, Tyler shows up and asks me to continue investigating Magnus. Not officially, but on the QT. Pays me money. Always a plus. About two hours later, your father calls me and wants me to investigate Magnus and a police officer."

"Deidre?" Nala guessed.

"That's the one."

"Didn't he want you to listen in to the recorded calls of all the guys he put away?"

"That one is unofficial business."

"What's the issue?"

He made a growly snort. "Should be nothing. The money is pouring in, but I'm getting a whole lot of nothing. Then something peculiar happened."

The word *peculiar* never did have good associations for her. "I'll bite."

"Tyler's clean. I think I already told you that. No coded conversations going on in the prison telephone conversations. A few are pretty strong in their desire to have more money put in their canteen accounts to buy more smokes and candy bars. Nothing much about Deidre, either. An ordinary girl who earned a few speeding tickets. That's all for her."

The elephant in the room was Magnus. "Last time we talked you told me Magnus was wiped clean. You called it a professional job."

"It was. I'm glad to hear you say that, too. I was hoping I hadn't dreamed it all because today Magnus has background information. An ordinary guy or gal couldn't get to it. There's some information about him originally being named John Wayne Walton and being a witness in a RICO trial. Before the change, he was in real estate. Even had some cosmetic work done since his visage was in so many real estate magazines."

Real estate agents could be bold. They had to be to push a sale. "I can see a real estate agent entering a cop bar. He could have been passing out some type of discount voucher when he met Deidre." It made more sense than a random guy walking into a bar because he saw an attractive woman through the window.

"I don't like it."

"What don't you like about it?"

"The name for one. John Wayne Walton. That's lazy. Whoever decided to make up the story was in a hurry. Didn't even try to make it sound ordinary."

"People name their kids after celebrities all the time. There was a guy running for dogcatcher named Elvis Presley Jones."

Elvin continued. "I know people name their kids after celebrities. It's all too convenient. Your client mentions her boyfriend's in the witness protection program and suddenly there's a buried entry about good old John Wayne Walton. Before you ask, no one would be stupid enough to put that information online. It would be in a closed system that no outsiders would have access to. This was put there for me to find after doing some mid-level hacking. I'm insulted that they had such a poor opinion of my skills."

The found information could mean many things, including Magnus actually *not* being in the program. "Do you think they know it was you peeking?"

A car behind her honked as she idled at a light too long. Startled, she pounded the accelerator and zoomed forward. What a difference a couple of extra cylinders made. Her eyes were on her rearview mirror to see if the honker made it through the light when Elvin spoke.

"I have my signals scrambled, and I have a few bounce backs to keep things confusing. They might think the hacker is in Croatia or Romania. What they do know is there *is* a looker. Someone decided to give whoever was sifting through the digital debris just enough information to appear authentic. By the way, what I do is investigating, not peeking. That makes me sound like a grade school boy standing underneath the stairs trying to look up girls' dresses. I do not peek."

"Sorry. The information didn't work for you because it seemed too obvious?"

"That was my first impression, then I decided the syntax was all wrong. Sometimes the subject and verb were reversed. It sounds more like someone trying to translate something into English and making sure to cover all their bases. Gave the guy a name, a job, and a reason to be in hiding. But wait! He's not hiding. He's living with a cop."

"I found that part somewhat suspicious myself. Along with the fact he volunteered the information to Deidre. I always assumed people died with that type of information."

"Many times, if it gets out, they do die."

"Great." What should she do now? "Did you tell my father or Tyler?"

"I called them before I called you."

"You called them?" Her voice approached a screech toward the last word.

"They paid me upfront. Besides, you never came back and told me to keep on Magnus."

"It was assumed you would when Tyler asked you to."

"Don't play the game with me. You and Tyler are not a team. He didn't tell me to contact you."

"Well, he should have." Even though the transaction probably took place after the incident, she was still irritated that she hadn't been included in the information exchange. An uneasy tickle rippled up her spine and around her shoulders. Something dangerous was going down. There were too many contenders, including the missing in action Dog Park Romeo, Magnus, and possibly a disgruntled felon her father put away. Maybe even one of the folks collecting disability checks while racing go-karts and jumping on trampolines had it out for her. "Why are you calling me?"

An audible sigh sounded over the line. "This will probably get me in trouble, but I thought you should know. Both your father and your beau are the type to take care of the little woman. I, on the other hand, think the little woman needs enough information to take care of herself."

"I appreciate that." The fact that Elvin would risk ticking off paying customers signaled there was some danger involved. "Should I be worried?"

"Not exactly worried." He paused as if gathering his thoughts. "Just be careful. I doubt anything else will happen. Too many eyes are on you now, which makes it a much greater percentage of being caught. Don't take chances. Keep Max with you."

She cut her eyes to her canine pal, who sat up a little straighter. "He's not exactly an attack dog."

Even though she had returned her focus to the road, she still felt the disdain wafting off Max. Elvin kept talking. Obviously, the waves didn't carry through the phone. "It doesn't matter. He looks menacing."

"Menacing?" Max echoed the word in a slightly higher register.

"You say it like you never considered the possibility."

"Yeah, I do." Nala readily agreed, hoping to cover up Max's slip. "He's just a big lovable bundle of fur to me. Okay, I got it. Don't take chances. Be aware. Take Max with me."

"Good. I know you know this stuff. I didn't mean to alarm you. Gotta run. I'm fixing Amy a special dinner tonight, and I need to hit the grocery."

"Thanks for the heads up."

Nala waited for the screen to indicate the call had ended and the music to return before addressing Max. "We need to be hyper-vigilant. We're in the thick of it now."

"Hyper what? What's thick?"

Snickerdoodles! At least Max could look menacing.

Chapter Twenty

A BUZZ ON the intercom system and the breathless voice of Gwen Bonne sounded. "Let me in, dear. I brought you a surprise."

From her position behind Sawyer's desk, Nala groaned. Her mother didn't figure into her day. Things were almost back to normal, if she could consider her father on the hunt for a domestic terrorist who blew up her car as just another day. Added to that, her short time partner had left after he'd informed her of his plans to see the world with his friend he referred to as Demon Seed. The good news was she no longer had to wear a sling.

Max lifted his head slightly and regarded her with a quizzical stare. She knew what he was asking. Even though he could talk, a good part of the time all it took was a look, which implied *I'm getting up.*

However, with Mother, it was hard to know what she might be bringing up. "If we're lucky, it's an early lunch or a late breakfast. The fact she sounded breathless makes me wonder. Wouldn't put it past her to tote a perfectly appropriate single male up the stairs if she were strong enough."

She punched the release button and spoke into the intercom. "It's open. Make sure to close the door behind you."

Her burglar, who had broken into the building more than once, was behind bars. He and one of his felonious comrades had previously used her office for business of a questionable nature, which might explain his desire to get back into the office. When she moved in, she scoured the office from top to bottom without finding anything besides dust. Even though Toby, her frequent visitor, was incarcerated, there was no reason to leave the door open for any of his associates.

Nala glanced back at the desk where she'd been working. Sawyer implied he would be back. He just didn't know if it would be a few months or a few years. Apparently, good old Damien thought they could work their way around the world. Not sure if there was much need in other countries for an insurance investigator and accountant who didn't know the local language.

A long bay accompanied by the scrabbling of dog nails and her mother yelling, "Slow down, Buster!" indicated a free meal was not in the offing. Max surged to his paws, nose pointed in the direction of the door and grumbled, "I don't like the sound of this!"

"Me, either."

Her mother was convinced the reason she hadn't pinned down the Dog Park Romeo was because they were going about it wrong. The scammer wasn't interested in relatively young women. The *relatively* part needled her. She might not be a college coed, but she wasn't ready for the geriatric unit, either.

A scratching on her recently painted door had her reaching for the handle as her mother, on the other side, needlessly announced, "We're here."

A large bloodhound pushed through the opening, pulling her

mother in the process. "Buster! Buster Brown, stop! We're here."
The dog didn't stop. Instead, he circled the room, baying, which
caused Max to bark. The hair on his back stood up, which meant he
felt threatened. Not a good sign. Rushing footstep sounded, then
Harry rushed in through the open door.

"What's going on?"

Nala shouted to be heard over the dogs. "I haven't a clue." She
nudged Max with her leg. "Stop it."

The baying continued as the large dog sniffed around the room,
knocking papers off a desk and wiped out the entire coffee pod
collection with his tail. Nala ran after the pair picking up items.
"Can't you get him to stop?"

"I've tried," her mother insisted. He's on a scent. He picked it up
when he entered the building."

"Snickerdoodles!"

"No need for such language, young lady," her mother managed
to breathlessly reprimand her.

Nala grabbed onto the leash creating more drag, but Buster in
full sniff was a formidable creature and still managed to tug the two
of them along. Harry joined them on the leash, pulling the dog to a
stop.

"My uncle had a bloodhound. What you need to do is to inter-
rupt the scent. I've got some chewing tobacco in my office. I'll go get
it."

Nala wrinkled her nose. *Chewing tobacco.* Maybe that's the real
reason Karly started the slow fade on the man. As soon as Harry let
go, Buster pulled toward the open door of the inner office.

Her mother was already flushed and breathing hard. This had to be hard on her. "Mother, let go. It's not like there's much more he can do to the office. You let go and close the hall door. I'll hold on."

When her mother let go, Buster surged to the open inner office door and knocked over the dog statue. He promptly sat and bayed.

A thoroughly mussed Gwen Bonne came to stand by the howling dog and shook her head. "I never liked that statue, either, but I didn't go all crazy on it."

Nala had regarded the statue as whimsical—not high art. When the building supervisor told her the previous occupant of her office had left without paying and the contents of the office loitered in the basement, she and Harry went down to investigate. Since the super had long since given up on holding the contents as ransom for back rent, he'd informed the two of them to take whatever they wanted.

Her hope was to find a reason for the break-ins. Instead, she'd found discarded furniture and the dog statute. There were no paper records, which she should have expected. Harry snagged some furniture for his office, while she took the dog statue knowing good and well it would annoy her mother's refined taste. Something about it spoke to her.

Max padded over to the bloodhound and the statue. He sniffed at the statue and barked. "Not you, too," Nala spoke, then held her fingers to her lips. Recognizing the signal for silence, Max barked no more, but stood and glared at Buster as if to say there was only room for one dog in the office.

Harry opened the outer door and came in waving a small circular tin. "I found it. One of my distributors left it behind. All you do is wave it in front of the dog—" He stopped, staring at the dog sitting and baying. "He's found whatever scent he was on."

"I, for one, was not looking for kitschy, animal statues." Her mother sniffed with a slightly superior air. "Can we get him to stop?"

Harry's brows knitted together, then he stepped forward and picked up the statue. Buster stopped baying and looked up at him with an expectant expression. Harry placed the can on a nearby table, then fished out a jerky treat he tossed to Buster who gobbled it up.

Max yipped, possibly upset that not only had Buster taken over the office, he was getting the dog treats.

Harry's hand dipped back into his pocket and retrieved another treat. "I didn't forget you."

As he held out the treat for Max, Buster snapped it up.

"Your dog has no manners, Mother. Where did you get him?"

Her mother managed a weak smile. "I had no clue he'd be so hard to handle, being retired and all. Henry Albert, IPD dog trainer, took Buster after he was retired. As you know, I'm friends with his wife, Helen."

"I doubt Henry would let you take Buster. Trained dogs need a handler. Do you know what he was trained to find?"

There was a slight hesitation as Gwen mulled over the matter. "I think bombs."

The two of them gave the dog statue a speculative look. The statue slipped from Harry's grip to the floor as Nala closed her eyes. Not exactly the ending she was hoping for. There was so much she hadn't done. If it was the journey and not the destination, it had been a mighty short trip.

A crunch of splintering pottery, then a long bay from Buster. Inside the shards of the pottery dog was a cloth bag. Nala knew enough to swoop in and pick up the bag before Buster could. Sometimes, drug dogs could destroy the evidence if the handler wasn't fast enough. The bloodhound lunged for the bag only to be stopped by the solid body of Max.

Nala emptied the sack on the table while Max kept Buddy at a distance. There were dozens of brilliant green stones and some small bags of white stuff. Gwen picked up a stone.

"Emeralds. I never heard of a jewel finding dog." Her mother used a finger to push a bag of white powder around. "Oh, that's right. Buster is a drug-sniffing dog."

It was hard to believe that had been sitting in her office without her having a clue. It was obvious that Max was not a drug-sniffing dog. "We need to call Dad and Henry to pick up his dog."

Her mother held up her index finger. "This time I have to agree with you. Could you not elaborate about my part in this entire incident?"

"The part about your hijacking a drug dog?"

"Retired drug dog."

"He was probably retired because of his behavior. I'll say I don't recall when he asks how the dog managed to end up in this part of town, entered a locked building, and made it up three flights of stairs."

Nala picked up a few of the stones and gazed at them. "I'm betting this is exactly what my thief wanted."

Harry laughed. "No doubt. Life has been so much livelier since you opened your office. Still, I got work to do. There's a big demand for costumes."

With emeralds still in hand, Nala glanced up to show she did pay attention to Harry's business, which specialized in superheroes, monsters, and cult television shows costumes.

Her mother was the first to ask the obvious. "Is it that comic con thing?"

"Nope." He smiled, then added, "Valentine's Day."

Some things Nala was better off not knowing. All day she'd have to fight the mental image of dressing up like Wonder Woman or Tyler surprising her in a Thor costume. He could totally pull it off, though.

The out of control bloodhound went silent, drawing their attention as he lay down, rested his head on his paws and closed his eyes.

"Goodness," Gwen exclaimed and pushed her hands together. "He must be exhausted. I know I am." She strolled over to the crushed velvet love seat and sat. Her hand caressed the fabric. "At least this feels nice. You'll want to replace the loveseat as soon as possible with the money you get from the emeralds."

"Mother! *You* gave me the loveseat."

Her mother fanned herself and acknowledged her remark with a sniff. "I gave it to you to get it out of the warehouse. It pained me every time I saw it. Not surprised the client wouldn't take it after insisting on ordering it. One of the designers ordered it from one of those kitschy places that stock atrocious inventory and call it hipster. Maybe you got your dog statue from there?"

"Nope. Hauled it up from the basement. I assume it was somehow associated with the previous office. Apparently, Toby had no clue where the emeralds were hidden."

Before she could elaborate, her mother continued talking. *No surprise there.*

"Have you considered what you could do with the money from the emeralds?" Her mother held up a green gem to the light and turned it slightly.

For the tiniest second or two, she had. It would be wonderful to buy a new car, possibly invest in the investigator's wardrobe she needed to buy. The fact her office had been broken into many times and there were drugs mixed in with the gems meant it wasn't a fortunate find such as finding a painting or a rug a former owner left behind.

"It's obvious they're stolen, which makes them evidence." A tinge of regret tugged at her over having easy money slip through her fingers, but there was nothing easy about it. She wasn't even sure how gems were sold. Someone would recognize them as stolen, and they'd be returned to the original owner. The insurance company might be offering a reward, though.

"Please. I'm familiar with how this works. No one is getting a whole fingerprint off a stone unless it's The Hope Diamond due to its size. Besides, you already handled everything."

"Not really. I only dumped the bag on the table." She held out her hand with the stones. "And these stones."

Gwen squinted at the gem she held up. "If only I had Grandpa's Loupe, I could check this out better."

"What are you looking for?"

Her mother always had a fondness for jewels and insisted on her father's presents taking the form of jewelry and occasionally trips where they'd often picked up more wearable art, as her mother liked to call it. Nala never pointed out that wearable art could also refer to tattoos.

"Clarity, purity, color. I might even be able to see the scratches that were made when they pried the gems out of their setting. It would make them less valuable."

"You could do this with that little glass that jewelers put up to their eyes?"

Gwen gazed at the stone as she answered. "Mostly. Refraction is how light passes through it." She dropped her hand and blinked. "I have to admit it's hard seeing anything without my reading glasses. Emeralds are much more valuable than diamonds because there are fewer of them. Diamonds usually have a tiny mark that identifies them. It's to discourage diamond smuggling. I'm not sure if emeralds have such a mark."

Emeralds. She was familiar with the glittering gem, but there was something else about emeralds that she had forgotten. It had to do with this office. The iconic lightbulb switched on and she shouted, "I got it!"

"You got what, dear?" her mother asked.

Nala stabbed her finger in the direction of the scattered gems and drug bags. "The guy who kept breaking in. Dad told me he'd been arrested robbing a house during a party. The victims claimed he'd taken a bunch of stuff including furniture and a life-size portrait. Nothing was found, but I remember emerald jewelry was part of the missing items."

"Yes, I remember that. I know the family." She gave a cough. "The wife came into our store once and wanted to change up her entertaining area. We showed her several tasteful creations, but she wanted something over the top rather like a circus tent in her front room. At Posh Interiors, good taste is never out of style."

It was the store slogan, and her mother never missed a moment to quote it. Nala cut her eyes to the crushed velvet loveseat.

"Sweetheart, that is so unfair. I didn't pick out the loveseat. A client did. Still, it's not as bad up here as I thought it would be."

The intercom buzzer sounded. Nala strolled over to it while her mother spoke.

"Too soon. I haven't had a chance to figure out if they are real emeralds or fake."

"Isn't the fact that they were hidden say *real* to you?" She depressed the button and spoke into the intercom, "How can I help you?"

"Nala, it's your father and Henry."

"Okay. It's open." She figured it was him before he spoke, but there was no camera on the door. Always better to be suspicious, which sounded like the motto for a conspiracy organization.

"They'll run up here before I'm done examining the jewels. I'm almost certain they're fake."

"How would you know that, and what would be the point of hiding phony gems?"

Her mother's shoulder went up in a shrug. "People do odd things, but I'm betting they didn't know they were fake. As for them being fake, it's more about comparison. Fake shatters more easily. When light comes through a stone, it's refracted. Not so much with glass. Actual jewels are heavier than their imitations."

"What you need is an actual emerald for comparison."

"Afraid so. I have been working on your father, but I don't think I will get one in the next twenty seconds."

A knock sounded, which had Nala reaching for Buster's leash. "Come in!"

Her father and an older man she recognized as Henry entered, causing Buster to surge to his feet and wag his tail. Henry thanked Nala for sheltering his dog, then said his goodbyes as he led the dog away.

Her father noticed the gems on the table and approached. He didn't touch them. Instead, he knelt, so his eyes would be at table level. "This is why your office was being broken into."

"That's my opinion."

Max stood by her father, waiting to be noticed. Not to be left out, her mother pushed to her feet and strolled to the table. "Not sure why everyone is making such a big deal about fake emeralds."

Her father remained focused on the gems, but still asked, "How can you be certain?"

"You know my grandfather was a diamond cutter."

"You aren't."

"I did learn some things from him."

"Are you a hundred percent certain?"

Her normally confident mother stared at the floor. "No. It's hard to be sure when so many realistic counterfeits are coming out of Asia. You'll need an expert. Not a jeweler, but someone who evaluates gems for a living. A jeweler is merely a merchant."

"Fortunately, we have an expert we can call."

"Not a policeman," her mother exclaimed. It didn't take a mind reader to know she was about to object. Obviously, her father sensed it, too.

"No. An expert. We use him in all the jewel smuggling cases. Not that we have all that many in Indy. I'm calling it in." He turned to address Nala. "With your permission, of course, since they were found in your office."

No way she wanted to be associated with the included drugs. Nala's shoulders went up in a shrug as she felt the oodles and oodles of money slip through her fingers. "I would appreciate knowing if they are real or not."

Her father's lips went up in an understanding smile. "You can retain ownership of them as long as they're not stolen."

"Finders keepers, huh?"

"Exactly."

Nala dropped the gems still in her hand into the bag. "Goodbye new car. I know good and well jewels hidden in a statue have a ninety-nine-point-nine-percent probability of being stolen."

"Sorry, princess. You're right. I'll have to call in someone to bag the evidence. We usually have more than one officer present with evidence to establish the chain."

Her mother was like an automaton that had stopped in mid-action. Her mouth was open the tiniest little bit.

"Remember, Gwen, I don't show up in Posh Interiors and tell you how to do your job."

AFTER THE DETECTIVES arrived, bagged the evidence and her father left, her mother remained, sitting on the seat and not speaking. It was probably the first time her husband ever told her to mind her own business, even as politely as he had. While it was way past time for such a remark, she still felt sorry for her mother, who acted like she had no clue what to do next.

"Maybe you can help me on the Dog Park Romeo case."

Her mother glanced up with a spark in her eyes—just a tiny one that needed tending to bring back the mother she knew.

"I was thinking the con artist preferred mature women. They probably aren't as cynical as millennials."

Her mother gave a slow nod. Nala worried a little as if somehow her mother was broken. The only time she hadn't witnessed her mother going ninety miles an hour and certain she was in the right was when she had bronchitis, and that was a long time ago.

"You would have to use Max. He's the only dog I feel comfortable with you leading. Would that work?"

A smile transformed her mother's countenance. "I've researched the parks and know which ones would attract a wealthy clientele. I suspect your Romeo shows up during the day at your non-peak hours."

Just like that, she was back.

Chapter Twenty-One

ENOUGH DAYLIGHT STILL remained to justify going to a dog park. Trust fund babies, retirees, and shift workers could go to the dog park in the middle of the day. However, she didn't expect too many of the latter at the park her mother suggested. "Are you telling me you have to purchase a membership to use this particular park?"

Her mother patted Nala's shoulder. "Don't worry, sweetie. I'll pay for it. It's an annual fee to use the park all year."

Max sat by Gwen as they waited for Nala to lock the office. "I don't think they'll even let me into that part of town." As they walked, she asked, "What's with the fee, anyhow? Didn't you say it was attached to a boutique pet store?

"It is. Still, dog parks can get pretty worn without maintenance. Most of the folks on that side of town don't trust anything that doesn't have a membership fee. Too afraid they might rub shoulders with riff-raff. It's the perfect place for your scam artist. Women will assume any man there is part of their rarified community. Their guard will be down. Thank goodness Max gives the appearance of a full-blooded shepherd."

Normally, a remark about his mixed heritage raised his hackles. *Nothing.* Instead, his attention was consumed by the open door to Harry's office. Her pooch shot into the opening before she considered shouting *stop*. There was a yelp, then feminine laughter. Finally, Max emerged with his tail wagging. Karly stepped out into the hall.

"Hey, you two. Where are you heading?"

Even though Karly was well versed about the case, Harry wasn't, and she'd like to keep it that way. "Crime waits for no woman."

Her friend paused as she tried to work out the cryptic clue. "Okay, then. Harry invited me over to see which dog would be best for his office." Before she could answer, Harry popped out of the office and waved. "What dog should it be?

"I'm thinking Mimi. She's a senior dog, but small enough to carry if the stairs become an issue. She's no longer a puppy, which means she won't chew through your inventory. We should head down to the shelter and see if Mimi picks *you*."

"Good luck with that," Nala called out, holding up her hand in goodbye and heading down the stairs.

Since Karly was practically legendary with matching up pets and people, she wasn't worried that Mimi might not pick Harry. She wouldn't be surprised if Karly hadn't already been coaching the dog.

As they reached the outside, her mother turned to glance back at the building and shook her head. "Was she serious about the dog picking him?"

"Absolutely. Remember, you're now in the undercover world of indulgent dog owners. I'm not sure if other owners will attempt to talk to you, but if they do, the more overboard you are about Max, the more normal you will sound. The fact we are paying a fee to walk through a pet shop to use the dog park says it all."

"True enough." She cleared her throat. "Should I go with a Southern Belle accent? Y'all's dog is mighty handsome."

"No accent. That would be a dead giveaway. Be yourself."

"Should I use my own name?"

"Maybe not. Your husband is rather well known in the area, especially by those on the wrong side of the law. It doesn't help that I ended up in the paper, either. You need a different name."

"How is that being myself?"

"Act like yourself with a different last name. I doubt it will come up. Most people don't usually give their full name. It gives them the ability to vanish if needed without someone tracking them down." Nala held out her wrist to check her watch. It hadn't even been ten minutes, and she already regretted including her mother. She pointed to the large sedan. "There's the car."

"I recognize it. I should since I've driven it for the last three years." She clicked her tongue. "It's a shame you live in a world where people refuse to give last names."

Even though there was a temptation to go it alone, she had to wonder if maybe her mother was the right person for the job after all. Maybe her dog was correct. Her mother's know-it-all attitude would make the average man run for cover, but the scammer wasn't looking for a real date, just easy money. Con artists loved folks with vanity plates and know-it-all attitudes. It was easy to trick someone, who assumed everything was all about them, into *helping* a con artist. Her mother's attitude just might work in her favor. It might even help her fit in, but the difference would be that she wouldn't believe the lies the con artist would spin.

Nala's job would be to shop while keeping an eye on her mother. She also had the spy glasses that made her resemble the biggest nerd in the city or someone attempting to cosplay Clark Kent. The glasses allowed her to take photos by blinking. It had to be a hard blink, not a flutter. It would make her look like she was in constant pain. With the glasses, she was sure no one would be looking at her.

She pulled the key fob out and pushed it. The reassuring metallic click of the doors unlocking made her smile. Driving her mother's former car was a lot nicer than she expected. There was so much she'd done without to maintain her vintage ride. She could have said it was cheaper, but the repair bills said otherwise.

Max had to scramble into the back, since her mother would insist on riding shotgun. Her mother eased into the passenger seat, tucked her purse by the console, then swung her feet in together primly, held together at the ankle. Everything she did was so calculated to be elegant and lady-like, it made Nala wonder why she didn't have any of those affectations. Probably due to being at the shooting range with her father. Although her mother tried to teach her, she just couldn't recall any of it taking.

As Nala slid behind the wheel, her mother gave a slight nod. "I always give the gas a little tap before I start the car to get it ready."

This was how it was going to be. Her mother had a boatload of driving tips that didn't make much sense. They didn't hurt anyone, but they didn't help, either. Normally, she'd ask where such a gem of driving wisdom came from, but she didn't have the time. Instead, she made a show of touching the gas pedal before turning the car key.

"Nala, you did it too hard. Remember, just a tap."

"I'll remember." She checked her rearview mirror when a thought occurred to her. "Who taught *you* to drive?"

"My cousin, James."

"The practical joker," Nala clarified. She didn't see much of her extended family, but she did remember the hand buzzer and the whoopee cushion.

"Oh, he had his moments." Her mother's voice turned warm with remembering. "My father didn't have the patience to teach me to drive, and my mother didn't know how. I'm sure my father paid James to teach me, but still, it was awfully sweet of him."

"Yes, it was," she agreed, but was more interested in proving a theory. "Did he tell you about tapping the gas pedal before starting?"

"He did. However, your father insists newer cars don't need it."

It could be cars never needed it, and James was a joker to the end. Still, no need to ruin her mother's memory. "Probably so."

They made it across town with her mother only telling her twice to slow down—even though she was only two miles over the limit. There were six *watch out for that car*. Of course, she'd seen the cars, which was part of the reason she hadn't hit them. They were almost there, and with any luck, there would be no more helpful driving directions.

"Over there. On your left." Her mother waved her hand the direction she wanted Nala to turn.

A tasteful wood and stone building sat with a discreet sign that announced *Bark Boutique and Park*. Underneath the name was smaller lettering that said for members only. Personally, she thought the sign was confusing. It made it sound as if the store was for members only. A few luxury sedans and one pricey SUV sat in the parking lot.

"The SUV belongs to the owner," her mother announced. "I checked this out when I bought a membership. They'll expect to see me. I'll explain you're a friend."

"Okay, though not sure why you have to explain anything."

"Wait and see." Her mother swung her door open while Nala pondered her remark. Were they going to ask for ID as they entered? Her mother placed a small paw-print pin on her coat.

"What's that for?"

"The membership pin that allows you to use the park."

"All it takes is a pin?"

"And the fifty-dollar joining fee. Don't forget that part."

She hadn't forgotten, but her mother hadn't mentioned the actual amount before. Fifty dollars wouldn't be too much if the hunting was good. "Someone could buy a membership and allow their dog walker to use the pin?"

"I guess so. Would you like me to introduce you as my dog walker?"

Before Nala could answer, her mother's phone chimed. She slowly typed out a text with one finger.

"Who was that?"

"Your father. He wanted to know where I was. Peculiar. He never used to ask where I was."

How soon she forgot about the bloodhound incident or pretended to. "He's probably worried that you're out trying to steal another canine officer."

"You're as bad as your father. I merely borrowed the dog. I figured it would do Buster some good to get back in their field."

The door handle clicked as she released it. Nala turned toward the door to hide her smile. It amazed her how her parents had managed to live together so long, but obviously, it worked. Her feet touched the ground, and she stood and opened the back door to let

Max out. He exited the car with a leap and waited patiently for Nala to clip on his leash.

"I suppose I'm going to have to buy something here. What do you think the cheapest thing is?"

"Gourmet dog cookies."

"Got it. I'll be able to see you, but not hear you. What you want to do is schedule a date. Don't try to keep him talking after the date is made. His MO is he hits up the women for money after having an emotional meltdown because his dog is sick."

"Roger that." Her mother grinned at her.

She should tell her mother they didn't need to talk in code, since she wouldn't be able to hear her. If Nala got too close, she might scare off their Romeo. Then again, the man could have moved on, possibly to another city. They approached the store together, with Max walking with his head held high. He acted like he was in a movie, but she doubted their scammer would be suspicious of a dog's behavior. Before they even reached the door, it was opened for them by a slender man attired in a dog decorated sweater.

"Welcome. I see you have a pin. Dog park today?"

Her mother gave a superior sniff. "Do you think I would wear this cheap pin because I liked it?"

Hold the attitude, she wanted to remind her parent. This store owner could have a lot of information he didn't even realize. It might be best to wait and see how she was introduced.

Her mother made a slight nod in her direction. "I brought Samantha, my dog walker. I thought it would be nice for you two to meet. There won't be a problem with me using a dog walker, will there?"

Her words paired with her snobby attitude equaled more of a challenge than a question.

"Oh, no, ma'am. Many of our clients use dog walkers."

"Very well, then." She gave a regal nod as if she were the queen. "Samantha," she said, loud enough for anyone in the small store to hear. "I'm taking Max to the park. I so seldom get to take him for a walk on my own with so many important board meetings to attend."

"Yes, madame," she managed a little curtsey. Dog walkers probably didn't do that, but when her mother went all regal, she could out snob any duchess.

"You may look around. There is some," she took a deep breath as if it pained her to continue, "acceptable merchandise. I expect you to join me when you're done."

"Yes, I will." She didn't know if adding *madame* again would be overkill.

Max and Gwen exited through a door cleverly labeled park entrance. There was a good chance the other side of the door was park exit. Some nice sized windows allowed customers to view the park, which included an obstacle course and a small running track, plenty of benches, and small trees. Obviously, the park had been around a few years judging by the trees. It could even be the park had been built around the established trees.

An elderly lady walked two toy poodles with jeweled leashes. Nala assumed the gems were fake, which made her wonder about the emeralds in her office. Maybe there was a reward out for them. Any money would help. She didn't plan on driving her mother's old car for the rest of the year.

Gwen took Max one time around the running track at a sedate

pace. Then she sat down on a bench and fanned herself. It would be hard for anyone to believe her mother was hot in the winter. A younger man with an Irish setter addressed her mother. Her mother replied.

The man appeared average to her, not movie star good-looking. From this distance, she couldn't tell if his eyes were blue. A ruckus sounded behind her as the store owner greeted someone who tried to brush away the smarmy shopkeeper.

"Leave me alone. I'm not here to see you. I'm here to see Nala."

She froze, not daring to turn around. The male voice she didn't know, but the tone promised trouble. Her hand reached for her purse. She'd packed it before she left home. Instead of checking for lipstick and tissues when she got ready to leave, she made sure she had her mace, her siren, and her Glock. Since the gun fumble, she decided to put it a little deeper inside her bag. Her fingers encountered the plastic and metal siren. Effective, but it would be pointless since the man was already here. Mace would be her better alternative in a public place. She palmed the cylinder and pretended to wait as the man approached her. About that time, her mother turned and looked straight at her as if she could feel Nala's alarm. She mouthed the word *trouble,* hoping her mother would figure it out.

"Nala Bonne?"

Chapter Twenty-Two

THE BALD MAN wore a trench coat. The better to hide a weapon was Nala's first thought. Her second thought was he knew her name. "Pardon me, I don't believe I know you."

He stepped closer, and Nala put her finger on the top button of the mace can she had hidden by her palm. His dead eyes chilled her.

"You should. You have spent enough time combing through my records."

Nala sucked in her lips as she fought down a creeping sense of unease and mentally reviewed the cases she'd handled recently. The man bore no resemblance to any of the disability claims she'd taken over from Sawyer, probably because most of them were women. In no way should anyone know she was there. A faint memory surfaced of a side view shot of Deidre's mysterious boyfriend, who she claimed hated having his photo taken—fitting for someone in the witness protection program. "Magnus?"

"Give the lady a prize."

"Why are *you* here?" For a guy who was supposed to be keeping a low profile, he got around a great deal.

He put his hand in his pocket. "My father always told me if you wanted something done right you had to do it yourself. He handled explosives." The tips of his lips turned up in a smirk. "This is what I get for farming out work to idiots who can't calculate weight or pressure. Let's continue this outside."

"I think not." One of the first lessons her father taught her about survival was never go off alone with a stranger, no matter what. A chance a person could be killed in public was almost a certainty in private.

When he reached for her arm, she mashed down the nozzle on her mace can and pointed it toward his face. Not waiting to see the results of her action, Nala darted around a dog bed display.

The man cursed and rubbed his eyes. He floundered about yelling, "You're going to regret that. You must be a slow learner."

Well, she certainly hoped not. Her heart raced as her eyes darted around the store. There had been a few people in the store, but they must have fled or taken cover. It was just her and an enraged Magnus. Nala darted down the aisle in search of cover. It was hard to know what Deidre saw in the man. Maybe the truth might serve her.

"I quit investigating after Deidre told me to stop. I haven't done anything, especially after the explosion."

The man plowed through the pyramid of dog beds, forcing Nala to duck behind a display of dog leashes. The truth wasn't working out too well. Instead of reaching for her weapon, she snatched a dog leash with a heavy metal hook. She had no clue what happened to the other shoppers, but she couldn't take a chance of firing a firearm in a public venue, especially after already accidently discharging her weapon in the park. If that came out, along with firing inside a pet store, she'd lose her investigator's license and possibly do time.

"For a private dick, you don't even check to see if you're followed!" Magnus shouted the last part of the sentence as he barreled toward her.

A counter containing rhinestone studded collars—or at least she assumed they were rhinestone—sat behind Nala. The owner might be hunkered down behind it. She couldn't go any farther without endangering him. She'd have to stand her ground. The heavy metal clip of the leash she held would do damage if he took it full in the face. Even though she had doubts how effective it would be against a bullet, she swung it over her head in a circle, picking up speed.

As she calculated when to release the clip, she heard the sound of a door opening. Someone would be walking into danger. "Stay out!"

She swung the leash downward, catching Magnus on the side of the face. The man stopped for a moment, his eyes promising retribution as an angry welt pulsed on his cheek. It hadn't even brought the man down. What was he? First, mace, then the leash, but he kept coming. Her survival as well as the welfare of those in her immediate vicinity depended on her. Instead of panic, calmness came over her. She had this under control. Hadn't her father trained her to survive? The skillset she needed always existed in her mind.

The clatter of dog nails sounded, and Nala understood their significance. Her pooch was in the store, and she had another ally—not one she'd alert Magnus to. The chest-high shelving units would hide her dog.

"You're smart to keep bystanders out. I'll handle them after I take care of you."

He expected to kill her, then the others. She couldn't fail. All she had to do was keep the man's attention on her. "Why date a police officer?"

The man gave a bark of laughter. "Typical. Women are so easily tangled up in trivial details and romance. Remember, that was your last question." He brought up his gun and aimed it at Nala.

Max launched himself into Magnus at full speed, attacking from the side and throwing off his aim. The bullet went wild, shattering a window.

"What the...?" Magnus spun, trying to fight off the dog, but eventually stumbled to his knees.

His gun landed on the floor. Nala raced toward it with the intention of picking it up. When Magnus lunged for the weapon, she kicked it out of reach at the same time the man had his hand on it.

A bullet whizzed by, then a thud. No pain, so obviously she was still alive. Max had knocked down Magnus and his teeth were clamped around the man's right hand. For once, the man stopped struggling and glared at her.

Why had the man pursued her? She thought Elvin's results on the man were odd. Still, if a client didn't want her to pursue a case, she didn't. "What is it with you? I told you I stopped my investigation."

The exterior door opened and a smoke grenade was thrown in engulfing the room in smoke. "Hold," she instructed Max as she pulled her shirt up over her nose. It was a lot to ask of an animal whose scent capability was much better than hers.

"Police!" A masculine voice shouted. The identification eased her mind. For a moment, she thought Magnus had arrived with cronies.

"Over here. The suspect is being held courtesy of Officer Max."

"Bystanders?" The voice called out again as the smoke started to clear.

"Not sure." Nala answered. "There may be."

When the smoke cleared, four swat officers were visible, which seemed like overkill to Nala. Magnus wasn't on the up and up, that much she knew. Probably on the slightly illegal side, too, but she never thought swat-officer dangerous. Nala settled for pointing to Magnus. The officers rushed him, relieving Max of his task.

The store manager's head popped up just above the counter. "Is it safe?"

"I think so."

Her gaze swung to the park door, which stood open. Her mother rushed in brandishing a gun. "Drop your weapons! I'm armed and not afraid to fire."

The store manager's head went back down. The swat team went on the defensive, their weapons pointed at her mom. Good heavens! Who knew her mother was armed? "Mother! Put the gun away. The police already have Magnus."

Her mother put up her weapon, assumed a more upright posture, and the swat team relaxed, exchanging grins. Good thing they didn't react immediately to having a gun pointed in their direction and recognized their captain's wife. After cuffing Magnus, one officer read him his rights, and they walked him out of the store, with some nods and smiles to the women.

The store manager's gaze took in both women. "My business will never be the same after this." He gave an all-over shudder.

With the corner of the store trashed, Nala felt sorry for the store owner, but her mother scoffed when she said so. "Please. People love a good story. You'll have plenty of people swarming the place. Most of them will arrive with the pretext of buying something. The story will be featured on the news. Make sure they get a good shot of the sign. You couldn't pay for that kind of advertisement."

The store manager stopped his moaning to give Gwen interested attention. "I could make a promotion out of it. Was there a reason the man was following you?"

"Gwen. Nala." Her father called out as he entered the room. Her mother ran to him and gave him a tight hug. "Thank you for responding to my text so promptly."

That explained why the officers were there.

Nala up righted the leash display and was about to replace the one she'd used on the rounder. The manager jogged around the counter. "I'll take that." He held his hand out for the leash. "I'll make a display out of it. Not only a great looking leash but a protective device for the owner, too. Maybe you can come back and demonstrate how to use it."

Who knows? It might add up to some business for her. "I could come back maybe once or twice."

"Excellent." The man rubbed his hands together. "Bring your crime-fighting dog with you."

"Sure thing. Come on, Max." She scooped up her purse and located a business card, which she placed on the counter. "Gotta run."

She met her mother and father outside the store. The other police vehicles were gone and along with them, Magnus. "What's going on?"

Her father had his arm around her mother and held out his other arm to her. She walked to him and hugged him. "Glad you responded to Mother's text. I know Magnus wasn't on the up and up, but what do you have on the man?"

"Elvin discovered he was your go-to guy if you wanted a new identity. He wasn't exactly the type of guy you pay thirty dollars for an identification that bears no actual resemblance to you, but at least it proves you're over twenty-one."

"What does he do?"

"Apparently, he changes identifications for career criminals. He can even make international passports, and they are flawless. This isn't just a local crime. We'll have to call in the FBI."

"Why Deidre?"

"No answer yet. Sometimes the simplest answers are the best. He could have simply been attracted to a pretty woman. Then again, there could have been the thrill of operating right under the police's nose. I'll let you know as I go along."

"Good. I'd be curious to know why he took out my car."

Her father gave her shoulders a squeeze. "Ah, sweetie, the man was *trying* to take you out, but oddly, the bomb was triggered by a spark, possibly caused by a stray bullet. Tyler told me your gun was missing a round. Anything you want to tell me?"

She knew it would come out eventually. "I may need to start wearing a holster."

Her father agreed while her mother held up a slip of paper and waved it.

"Is that what I think it is?"

Her mother arched her eyebrows. "I was masterful. Joseph, the guy that talked to me at the dog park, didn't know what hit him. We have a date tomorrow at Matt the Miller Tavern."

Her father dropped his arms from both her and her mother's shoulders and crossed them. "Should I be worried?"

"Of course not," her mother cooed. "Joseph is attractive, but he doesn't have the strong character that you do." She gave her husband's arm a playful tap.

"No worries, Dad. I'll look out for her. *Joseph* was a new name. It makes me wonder if we're dealing with the same person."

"Keep me in the loop since I want to arrest this perp."

Nala bent down to pet Max, who nudged her leg, certain he had been ignored long enough. "No worries. I *want* you to arrest him."

Chapter Twenty-Three

TYLER AND NALA strolled down Center City Drive as the sun made its slow descent toward the west. Under normal circumstances, an evening spent with Tyler would be a pleasant one. It still could be pleasant if they nailed their Dog Park Romeo. Doubt besieged her, realizing it all ended up in her mother's hands.

"I appreciate your coming as my pretend date."

"There's no pretense about it. Since you picked such a popular restaurant, I'm grateful you went to the trouble to get reservations."

She giggled, which was out of character for her. "I had to make reservations for both us *and* Mom. I was specific in saying we wanted tables close together. We can only hope. Elvin took the recorder from Max's collar and made it into a bracelet for my mother to wear. Apparently, my mother is going to wear long sleeves to hide the atrocious object."

"Your mother is a good sport."

"Yes, she is. You gotta love her enthusiasm for everything."

"Including you."

She sighed as they approached the restaurant entrance. "Don't I know it. In high school, I considered my father an impediment to dating. He ran background checks on all my dates. If that wasn't enough, he followed us around in a squad car."

"He probably made sure to stay out of sight."

"No. He wanted my date to see him. Even went so far as to turn on the siren."

An employee stepped out into the cold air and held the door open for them. Inside, warmth twined around the white tableclothed tables where crystal goblets sparkled and tiny votives flickered. A receptionist attired in black smiled and asked their names. When Nala gave her the last name of Bonne, she led them to a table. On the way, Nala craned her neck so much to check out the room to see if her mother and her date were there that she bumped into the receptionist.

"Oh, excuse me."

"Sure," the woman said, but her tone announced her irritation.

Once they were seated, Nala checked her watch. She'd intentionally come early so she could be in place by the time her mother arrived. Their waiter showed up and asked if they would like a cocktail.

Before Tyler could answer, Nala did. "Just water. Thanks."

The man left them with menus that Nala barely glanced at as she continued to search for her mother. Where was she? Didn't she know she needed to be here before the guy? He could show anytime and think he'd been stood up. It probably happened all the time in his line of work.

"I have to wonder if this is all payback from the time, we went the burger place on Monon Trail, and I saw your dad working with Max."

She well remembered the incident. Instead of turning to address her date, she spoke with her eyes trained on the entrance. "I remember that well. You and Dad talking while I brought up the rear with Max. It looked like my father was *your* date."

Tyler coughed. "I don't quite remember it like that."

"You aren't me." He had no clue how much time she spent over-analyzing his actions.

"Hey, that was stupid of me. I like your father, will admit to wanting him to like me, and I was curious about his training methods with Max. It isn't hard to figure out he can discourage any potential suitor if he puts his mind to it. I figured it would serve me well to get your father on my side. Now I just get odd stares as if he's trying to figure out if he should kick my butt or blame me for upsetting his daughter."

His sudden abandonment made sense. A smile illuminated her face as she turned to face him. "That means a great deal to me."

"I'm glad." He reached across the table for her hand, but before he could grasp it, Gwen's signature laugh could be heard. Nala whipped around and whispered, "She's here."

"Okay, I get that. Aren't we supposed to be on a date? You're going to look mighty strange turned around all night."

"You're right," she agreed and took one final look. "Whoa! My mother is showing cleavage. I wonder what my father thinks about *that*."

"He probably suggested it."

She shook her head. "Obviously, you don't know Graham Bonne as well as you think you do. He'd never ask his wife to wear something provocative for another guy."

After all, he'd been her father much longer than he'd been Tyler's academy teacher.

Tyler's eyes danced with amusement like he'd heard a joke but wasn't sharing it. She reached across the table to nudge him. "What's so funny?"

"You. I guess everyone sees their parents a certain way. How would a woman who was meeting a younger man dress?"

"Well," she hesitated, since that situation had never happened to her. "I suppose she'd want to appear younger."

"How would she do that?" He arched his eyebrows.

"It depends. I've seen plenty of fifty-something women wearing distressed jeans with holes in them, which is something Gwen Bonne would never do. I guess in my mother's case, she would add an extra layer of mascara and a push-up bra."

"Probably with her husband's approval."

Now it was her turn to arch her brows. "Because he wants his wife to be attractive to other men?"

"Because he wants her to be successful in her undercover assignment. I imagine this fellow has hit lots of women with his line about the ailing dog. He needs to find a woman who's into him. Sure, accepting a dinner invitation is one. How the woman dresses is another factor."

Her eyes flickered down to her tunic, that had no plunging neckline, and coordinating leggings. She even added her dress boots since she heard the restaurant was a nice one. What did her clothes say about her? Were they let's-hang-out clothes? The ensemble was one she'd worn with Karly before. "How *should* she dress?'

He held up his hands, chest high. "Don't ask me about women's fashion. I believe if a woman is interested in a man, she'll wear whatever makes her feel good and plays up her best features."

Her outfit passed the made-her-feel-good test. She wasn't sure about bringing out her best features. What was her best feature? Karly would claim it was her hair while her father would insist it was her mind.

"The perp is here," Tyler hissed the words.

"How do you know?" She made an effort to twist to see, but he leaned over the table and cradled her head in his hands. His unexpected actions surprised her and made her temporarily forget about catching a glimpse of her scammer. Tyler's lips touched hers gently, then he released his hold, resuming his seat.

"Remember, we're on a date."

That was their cover story, that much she knew. The real question was, was the kiss part of the story, solely Tyler's idea, or a little bit of both? "Can I look now?"

"You can."

She twisted in her seat to survey the people around them. No Mom or scurrilous con artist. "I don't see them."

Tyler held up one finger. "I was going to say that you could look, but they passed when I kissed you. They went deeper into the restaurant."

"Gingersnaps! I specifically told them when I made reservations our tables should be close to one another."

Tyler's shoulders went up in a shrug. "You know how it goes. The person you talk to is not always the same person who seats people. As far as I could tell when we walked in, the tables around us filled up fast."

So far, nothing was working out the way she'd planned, except the man had actually showed. "I need to go to the restroom." She stood and picked up her purse.

"What do you want if the waiter comes back?" Tyler asked, appearing a tad skeptical of her excuse.

"Whatever. Ask the waiter what's good. You order for me."

The crow's feet at his eyes crinkled as he asked, "The same way you decided I wanted water?"

"That will work." She turned in the direction her mother and her date went. Should she walk purposefully as if she were going back to her table? Since she had never been in the place before, she had no clue where the restrooms where. Better yet, she could be a person without their glasses or a drunk person without her glasses. No, that would be too much. She would be attracting too much attention.

Her steps were slow as she made her way through the rapidly filling restaurant. Most conversations were low-voiced, allowing Nala only to hear a word or two. One man spoke into his cell phone while his companion glared at him. It was obviously a business call, during what should have been his personal time. She had a feeling things wouldn't go well for him later tonight.

Wasn't she guilty of the same thing? Asking Tyler to be her date while she tried to keep an eye on her mother? Most people looked up to her mother because of her determination to do anything. Quite frankly, she was fairly sure her mother didn't consider she had *any* limitations. While Nala appreciated her help, the world of deceit and cons wasn't her mother's forte. Unlike Nala's clients, who'd had no clue they were being duped, her mother knew what was going on. In a moment of inspiration, Gwen had decided to bring a checkbook from a defunct checking account.

Her mother's sparkling laugh sounded again. She was fairly close. Joseph, as he was currently calling himself, probably thought he was charming her mother due to her laughter. He had no clue it was her fake laugh. Growing up, she heard the fake laugh so often she didn't recognize the deep, full-throated laugh that resulted in being deliciously tickled by something.

A man with a rather shaggy haircut leaned toward her mother. All she could tell from her quick glimpse was he wore an oxford shirt and had no beard, which made it an oddity in the current culture. There was no real way to tell if he resembled the guy from the television show, young or old.

An employee approached with menus tucked under her arm. "Excuse me," she flagged the woman down, "Could you point me in the direction of the restrooms?"

The woman pointed in the direction she was headed. She thanked the woman. Inside, she gave herself a mental high five. It would be perfectly logical to pass the table again on her way back and get a better look at the fellow, but only after she spent an appropriate amount of time in the restroom.

INSIDE THE RESTROOM, she stood around until another diner asked her if she was waiting for someone. Not knowing what to say and not wanting to appear a stalker, she mumbled something about waiting for a guy to pop the question.

The woman gave her a pat on the arm. "Young love," the woman enthused. "What I wouldn't give to be forty, again."

How old did the woman think she was? Nala rushed over to the mirror and smoothed out a couple of worry lines, then renewed her lipstick and patted the shine off her nose. Time to check out Joseph, and see what Tyler had ordered her for dinner. Since she knew her destination, her stride was long until she neared her mother's table. Then she took about a second or two of being in slow motion. The back of her mother's head came into view, then the guy. Odd, he didn't look particularly untrustworthy. Karly, who liked to associate people with dogs, would have called this one a *golden*, after golden retrievers—one of the friendliest dogs on the planet.

Blonde hair, open face, and boy, was he young. Was that a tear in his eye? If so, he could cry on command, which would make him convincing. She walked past. Stopping and staring would never work.

As she came around the corner to where she and Tyler were sitting, a woman blocked her way. Nala could hear the conversation. "It's nice to see you out. How are you going to know the town if you don't socialize more?"

Fig bars! A girl couldn't go to the bathroom and not have her date stolen out from under her. Nala cleared her throat, causing the woman to spin around gracefully. The tall blonde gave her a smile. "Sorry, I didn't see you there."

It's not a remark about your height, she reminded herself, then took a deep breath. "I'm back now." She was proud of herself that she didn't add *go back to your cave or wherever you crawled out from*. It would have been some place much more glamorous than a cave.

The woman gave a dainty finger wave, then left with a swaying walk on her knife blade heels to who knows where. There were probably other men for her to socialize with.

Tyler gestured in the direction the blonde went. "Layna's some socialite or bigwig, maybe both. She was at that auction the city did a while back."

There had been auctions, but she wasn't sure why both Layna

and Tyler would be at the same one. "Why were you there?"

"I was lending Callahan moral support."

The name sounded familiar, but she couldn't place a face to it. "Was my father there?"

He had picked up his water and took a sip when she asked. The questioned caused him to sputter and swallow with some difficulty. "No. Your father is a fine-looking man for his age. and I believe they even asked him, but he said no."

Fine-looking man? This evening had taken a turn at weird and kept on going. What could Callahan have been doing that involved being good looking? "First Responders Calendar Auction?"

"That's the one." He picked up his glass for another sip.

She tilted her head to one side and asked in a teasing manner, "What month are you?"

"No month."

"I can't believe they didn't ask you. They usually asked everybody. It's not the thrill most people imagine. Most wives and girlfriends vetoed the idea. Then they came after the guys that have no significant other to say no." Nala continued, "Why didn't you? Shy?"

He reached for her hand and rubbed his thumb along hers. "You think I'm shy?"

"Good question. I know you're not afraid to do your job whatever it might be. Still, at the same time, you're not a person who wants a lot of attention."

His other fingers wrapped around hers. "You are quite the private eye. You're right."

Silence stretched between them as they held hands and stared into each other's eyes, not wanting to disturb the delicate tension that existed between them.

"There you are!" a woman called out. Nala turned her head to see the woman from the restroom heading her way. "Let me be the first to congratulate you." She nodded to Tyler, then turned and simpered at Nala. "You're the lucky one. Enjoy."

She waited until the woman left, withdrew her hand from his and said, "You don't want to know."

"Okay."

His answer surprised her. Anyone else would insist on knowing what that had been about. Then again, he guessed she'd probably tell him in time. "What did you order for me?"

"I got two entrées. The Miller Burger and The Chicken and the Egg. The burger has regular fries and the chicken has sweet potato fries."

Nala responded, "Which one would you like?"

"Ha! I knew you'd do that. I made sure to order two things I'd like so no matter what you picked, I would win."

"Smart thinking." Nala complimented him, noticing his eyes sparkled when he was amused. No wonder blondie was trying to talk him up, but he was *her* date for the night.

"Every now and then, I come up with a good idea. I may have pushed Deidre your way just to start talking to you, but I'm so glad I did. Deidre's grateful, too, but right now she's just embarrassed because there will always be some people who will wonder how much she knew about Magnus and his identity changing business."

The poor woman. Most would think she was dirty when all she wanted to do was find a decent guy to call her own. "What's she going to do?"

"Talked about relocating to Atlanta, Georgia. That's where her folks are."

"That should be far enough away." It would take a while for the rumors to reach there, and maybe she'd have built up some credibility by that time. "I feel for her. It's hard to find a nice guy."

Tyler held out his arms. "What about me?"

"Jury's still out. I don't know enough about you yet." She reached for her glass, knowing the comment would rattle his cage a bit.

"You Bonnes are all hard asses," Tyler joked.

"Excuse me." A familiar male voice sounded behind Nala. She didn't need to see Tyler's flushed face to know who it was.

"Dad, I should have known you'd be around."

He took one of the extra chairs at the table and sat to be out of the way. "Elvin and I were out in the car listening in when your mother's date confessed to being in a dog walking ring that bilks little, old ladies out of their savings. Apparently, your mom's date is the weakest link. He told your mother she reminds him of his mother, and he felt bad about conning her. He even started crying and said he just wanted out. You know your mother. She told him she could make that happen. I'll be taking his statement, and we'll see what kind of deal can be worked out."

"With repayment to my clients," Nala reminded.

"Of course."

Nala reached for her purse. "I need to go with you."

"No, you don't. You've been in the police station before and witnessed how long everything takes. Eat your dinner. For a few minutes don't think about work, either of you. After dinner, come on down."

"Graham." Her mother said her father's name as she approached, guiding her date with one arm around his waist. "Joseph and I were waiting, but you were taking forever."

Her father stood. "Let's roll."

Nala watched the three of them leave together. "Do you think everything will be all right?"

"At least for the hour it will take to consume our meals."

That's one thing she liked about Tyler. He didn't sugarcoat. The waiter arrived with the meals. She took the burger, which was amazing. She gestured with a fry. "You know the only thing that could make this night even better?"

"Max. If Max was here."

"You read my mind. You do know we will have to order something for him. I can't go home smelling like a burger and not have something for him. I will get the dog guilt eyes I discovered are even worse than the I'm-so-disappointed-in-you parent eyes."

"No problem, I'll take care of it now." He held up his hand to get the waiter's attention.

Chapter Twenty-Four

SOME OF THE icicles had melted from the restaurant overhang while others were in full drip. Nala shouldn't expect much since it was only February. Karly had her hand on the car door handle as she turned to speak. "You never gave me the low down on the Dog Park Romeo case."

Even the thought of the case caused her to melt back into the comfy upholstery. "Whoa. That was a case and a half. There was an entire ring of dog walkers conning women."

"Really?" Karly turned her attention away from exiting and swiveled her body toward Nala. "Good looking guys, I bet."

"Hard to say." Nala shrugged. "I only saw Joseph. Ordinary enough. Definitely not the ones my client met. Even though he made a date with my mom, he couldn't complete the con and ended up confessing because my mother reminded him of his own."

Karly hooted. "That's rich! What about the other guys?"

"Joseph rolled fairly easy. Named names, including the ringleader. They even kept a file of their cons. The women. The parks. The cons. To make sure there were no repeats for at least two months. That's why they used multiple guys and different dogs. No one would ever describe the same guy."

"Clever in a twisted way." She tapped her fingers on her temples.

"They must have already used the park we tried and had moved on."

"Could be," Nala agreed. The memory of her mother calling her *relatively* young had her twitching her nose. "Personally, I think it's our age. Someone our age would think nothing of a twenty-something guy talking to us in the park. He wouldn't have us pulling out our debit cards in a hurry to give him money."

"Money. Yeah, since the both of us are loaded."

Laughter filled the car as they both got a good chuckle out of it. Karly wiped a tear away. "Oh my. If I had money, I would not be giving it to some stranger. There are plenty of pets at the shelter I would help first. It's been my experience most veterinarians will work out a payment plan for pet owners."

Yeah," Nala said. "If I had thousands in the bank, I would buy a car."

Karly patted the car console. "Not sure what you have against this car. It's a pretty sweet ride. You have to admit it doesn't stick out like a sore thumb."

As much as she hated to admit it, her friend was right. The luxury of stomping down on the accelerator and getting actual speed as opposed to hesitation was a very big perk. "It has its good points."

"Oh please." Karly pressed the door handle until it clicked and swung her door open. "That's the kind of attitude you have when you talk up a guy you rejected to another woman. Oh, he has his good points. He's living and has all ten fingers and toes."

"Come on, when did I ever push my rejects on you?"

"You couldn't because you talked about them too much. I knew all the dirt."

"True enough," Nala swung her own door open. "I hope none of the employees are taking a smoke break and see me getting out of the car."

"Yeah, I guess your blind woman act wouldn't cut it."

"It's the only way to get Max inside. We could order to go, then just take it home." As soon as she said the words, she knew that's what she wanted to do as she pulled her car door closed.

Karly closed her door, too. "It looks like its take-out."

The two of them hovered over Karly's smartphone, deciding on their order. Max propped his head on the back of the seat. "I want chicken if they have it."

"Not chicken." Nala groaned. "I'll have to pick it off the bones."

"Whine, whine." Max chanted. "Didn't I save your life back at the dog park?"

"Ok, I'll give you that. Chicken it is."

Karly patted Max but spoke to Nala. "Whatever happened to that Magnus guy?"

"Oh, him." Her eyes lingered on the tiny print of the phone, deciding what she'd get. Only a nudge from her friend reminded her she hadn't answered the question. "The Feds took over the case. Turns out he committed numerous crimes by aiding and abetting known criminals by helping them slip out of the country."

"Yeah, that's bad. I guess the good thing is you're okay. I would almost pity the guy if anything happened to you." She shook her head and her lips formed a grim line. "I'm sure your father would go medieval on him. So, in a way, Max saved you *and* your father."

Max touched his cool nose to the back of Nala's neck. "Did you hear that? I'm a hero. I think I deserve chicken and steak"

"Really? I'm not sure I can afford my medical bills, and you want steak?"

"My bad." Max slunk back into the back seat and put his head on his paws.

Karly made a sympathetic coo. "Look at him. He's sad. I'll pay for his lunch. Too bad you couldn't use one of those emeralds you found to pay for stuff."

For a very brief time, she'd thought she might get a reward. Many insurance companies do offer a reward for information that will lead them to the missing item. Most rewards were at least a thousand dollars. Mentally, she'd already spent the money.

"That would have been nice. It turns out my mother was right. They were paste. The original owners were slapped with a class E felony charge and told to make restitution to the insurance company for monies they paid out."

Karly whistled. "That's ballsy of them, knowing all along they were paste."

"I would have gone with stupid. I guess in the jewel robbery business, it helps if you can tell the real from fake. I told my dad to pass along the information to the dude who kept breaking into my office."

Karly did a double take. "He knows him?"

"Only in a professional way. Since he's back in prison, it would be easy enough to relay the information." That would be one less thing for her to worry about.

"I'm ready to order. What do you want?"

"Pulled pork sandwich with a side of green beans. Max wants chicken, of course, without the sauce. No sides" She heard a whimper in the back but refused to acknowledge it. She waited until her friend called in the order to ask the question that had been nagging at her. From her friend's cheerful demeanor, she thought she could guess at the answer.

Karly ended the call and said, "They'll text us when it is ready."

"Speaking of ready—what's happening with you and Harry and Mimi?"

Her friend poked Nala. "Terrible transition. You were practically vibrating, waiting to ask me."

Typical of her friend to dance around the question and not answer it. "So?"

"I expect if you go to work tomorrow you should hear the clatter of dog nails."

"Woo hoo!" Nala fist pumped the air. "I knew it. You two are so stiff-necked that you refused to see the obvious."

Karly whooped with amusement. "You're calling *me* stubborn. Have you looked in the mirror lately?"

Her bestie never held back on home truths, especially when they were about Nala. Whatever it was, it was probably true. "Okay, I'll bite. What was I so stubborn about?"

"How soon you forget?" She chuckled, then smirked. "Tyler, of course."

"How so?" As she recalled, the moment she met the officer, she fell under his spell. There were just a few obstacles in the way.

"Ha!" Karly nudged Nala about the same time the phone chimed. "Our food is ready." She grabbed her purse and swung out of the car to get the order.

Nala called after her, "Make sure you remember what you were going to say."

The door slammed, and Nala spoke more to herself than to Max. "I'm not sure why she's talking about my being stubborn."

Max slid his snout onto Nala's shoulder. "Confusing. That's what I'd call you and Tyler."

"What do you mean?" She rolled her eyes upward as soon as the words were out of her mouth. No way would she take romantic advice from her dog. Still, he told things the way he saw them unless it came to food or hunger, which he tended to exaggerate.

"You like him. He likes you. I can smell it."

The thought of her pheromones flying everywhere didn't please her. Nala liked to think of herself as being more discreet. "That's true. It takes more than that, though."

"Please." He lengthened the word, possibly imitating Karly. Max was a fair mimic.

"Go on." She encouraged him, hoping for great insight.

"That's it." He gave a little huff as if she should know as much.

"No, that's not it. It takes more than that to make a relationship."

Instead of answering, Max stretched out in the comfy back seat, which caused the guy getting out the car next to her to give her an odd look. No reason for him to act like that. She could easily be on blue tooth or talking *at* her dog.

Karly returned with some appetizing smells and an inquisitive look as she opened the door. "What were you doing that caused that guy to give you the fish eye?"

"Nothing. I was talking to Max who decided to lie down, which made it look as if I was arguing with myself."

She gave a nod as she settled into her seat. "That explains it. Should I ask what you were arguing about?"

"Close the door and I'll tell you."

The door slammed, and Nala started the car. "Max thinks it's enough to like someone. He can't figure out why Tyler and I have so much trouble."

"Not trouble, exactly." Karly pursed her lips and wrinkled her nose. "I think it's more like you have more reasons not to date someone than to date them."

Thank goodness she hadn't started driving. It allowed her the opportunity to give her friend a hard look. "Really? *Miss, I can't trust him unless he owns a dog* girl."

"I didn't say I wasn't guilty of doing the same. Just think about it. First, you're hesitant because of his name, Goodnight, which does sound like it's straight from a romance novel."

"Yeah," she agreed with a sigh and backed out of the parking spot. "He could have had a last name like Butt or Hogg, which wouldn't be too cool being a cop."

"True. Then, you were worried over Tyler being a cop that your father would be in your business and all."

She cleared her throat since Karly overlooked the obvious. "My parents were already in my business. They invited him to Sunday lunch before we even went on a date. Then, my dad was always talking Tyler up like he's his agent, until I decided not to see him. According to Tyler, he was under a microscope with my father wanting to know what went wrong. My dad is not subtle"

"You have to admit some pregnant chick hugging him and saying something *about thank goodness she found him* was a tad suspicious."

After executing a turn out of the parking lot, Nala wagged a finger at Karly. "You told me I was justified in being suspicious."

"That's what friends do. I also pretended to like Jeff, but I never did. What was the fallout on the pregnant chick?"

"She was the wife of a military officer he'd served with. Apparently, the husband didn't make it back, and the wife had some issues with the VA. Tyler had told her if she ever needed help, he was there for her. She hadn't intentionally hunted him down, but she was visiting her sister when she saw us. She was all teary-eyed and hugging on him. Maybe I did get the wrong impression."

"Did you allow him to explain at the time?"

No, she hadn't. At the time, it seemed to her that Tyler's past had come to visit. "I did not. Come on, did you forget you were on my side?"

"Once again, need I remind you friends take their friend's side of the argument?"

Karly was starting to sound like a broken record. "I jumped to conclusions. Remember, he jumped to conclusions first, thinking I was involved with Elvin."

Laughter filled the car as they both got a chuckle at the thought. "Shows he didn't know Elvin very well," Karly concluded.

"Anyhow…" Nala smiled as she thought of the handsome officer who'd caught her eye and her heart, "…things are working out now."

"Ooh. Is it serious?"

Nala shrugged. "Don't know. I do know I'm going to enjoy the journey and not worry about the destination."

Max pushed his head between the seats. "Could I just have a bite? I'm starving. BTW, if you had listened to me, you could have avoided all these misunderstandings. The nose never lies."

The End

Cakewalk to Murder

A Painted Lady Inn Mystery

Chapter One

T HE JUDGES STROLLED to the next baker who stood proudly by a five-layer cake dusted with cocoa and decorated with live violets.

"This is the one," Donna declared and scooted up in her wing chair to be even closer to the television.

Her college-age helper, Tennyson, stroked his scruffy beard. It was a fair imitation of her husband, Mark, when he was in his contemplation mode. Ten dropped his hand and shook his head. "I don't know. What about Alastair? He used all those egg whites to make his cake lighter.'

"Please." She lengthened the word, then gave a derisive snort.

"That's so old fashioned. My great grandmother did that. Judges wanted something new, cutting edge, while still bringing indescribable joy to their taste buds."

"You think putting flowers on a cake will do it?"

A door sounded in the distant before Donna could reply. Currently, there were no guests in the inn and she had locked all the doors so she could have peace while watching The British Bake-Off Show. Unfortunately, she couldn't lock out Tennyson who had taken an interest in the program.

Jasper, her aging puggle, gave a welcome bark. It meant Mark was back from his Chamber of Commerce meeting, which he agreed to attend so Donna could watch the show in real time. If she recorded it, Janice would ruin it by calling her up, telling who the winner was and would make all these comments as if she had actually seen the show, too. No, thank you.

The judges talked amongst themselves as the tension built. Often, she imagined herself on the show and what she would make to tempt the finicky judges. The contestants must be nervous. Strangely enough, Donna was, too. A throw pillow found its way into her hands and she squeezed the pillow as the judges mentioned the third and second place finishers. They might have called them winners, but almost everyone conceded there was only one winner.

"And the winner is..." The lead judge paused for a moment. "Alastair! With his lighter than air Angel food cake. It reminded me of my dear old Granny and her ability to make every moment special."

Disgusted, Donna tossed the pillow in the direction of the television. It fell short by a few inches. "I can't believe it!"

This was so wrong. Tennyson laughing his fool head off didn't help, either. She turned to tell him so and discovered her husband standing in the entrance with a secretive smile. What was up with that? The half dozen Chamber meetings she attended didn't make her smile. Whenever there was more than one person on a committee, there would be endless arguments. Last time, the florist suggested they needed town colors. That took ninety minutes of her life that she would never get back.

Mark knew how to work a room and he waited a full minute until he had their attention. "I bet I know something else you won't believe."

It was hard to tell if her husband was teasing or not. He did deadpan so well. "Gary Manson, the owner of the music store, thinks Legacy should have its own song?"

"Yes. He's working on it, too. But, that's not it. It's something else. Something you might like. In fact, I know you'll love it!"

Her husband could be thoughtful, especially with it came to creative gifts. This one might be the best. She pushed up out of her chair and hugged Mark tight. "You're the best husband in the world!"

"I haven't even told you yet."

"No need. I know."

"How could you?"

Her euphoria dimmed a little as she got a tiny twinge that possibly her husband and she were not on the same page. "You were going to tell me you were going to attend all future chamber of commerce meetings without me? You're so much better at that kind of thing and they love seeing you there."

"No."

Donna dropped her arms and stepped back. "Then, what was

it?"

"As you know, we're always trying to bring business and tourists to Legacy to keep the town afloat."

Donna sighed. "Not another Gen Con. Last time, we had a dead guest."

"No. It's something you would really, really like."

Well, that was a puzzler. Somehow it involved business coming to Legacy. "It's a convention of handsome television sleuths with accents."

"Close." His eyes danced with mischief.

The man could keep this up forever. "Just tell me. I'm already upset that Alastair won the Bake-Off with his stupid Angel food cake."

"That's it!" Mark announced with a wide grin.

"Alastair coming here with his smug little attitude. Tell me no!"

The thought had her collapsing back into the wing chair while groaning. Tennyson laughed, again. Another throw pillow was in reach, which she lobbed at her helper. This time she hit her target.

"I can't believe it's so hard to tell you good news. Personally, I'm surprised you don't already know. Between your mother and Janice, you know if someone has a cold before their first sneeze."

Even though it wasn't her goal to know everything that went on, she knew a fair amount. Even to the point of her detective husband asking her questions about various cases when he had nada. "Haven't talked to mother today or Janice. She should have been at the meeting, too, but probably begged off to watch The Bake-Off Show. "Tell me. Now. I'm not the type of person who wants to keep guessing. I don't think anyone is."

Tennyson waved as if in class. "I like to guess. I bet America's

Next Top Model will be filming here."

"Another close one," Mark sang out.

"No Alastair." Donna shook her finger at Mark. "No models. Remember the part about you saying I would like it."

"You will." He chuckled, "But I better tell you before you're totally out of charity with me. As you know, the British Bake-off Show is very popular."

She nodded, not sure where he was going.

"Anyhow, American television producers want to have a similar show. They also want a quaint village-like town. Nora, the florist, entered our town into the running. She made some video about Legacy. Her son-in-law who works at the television station edited it for her. We watched it at the meeting and it did look good. Anyhow, Nora got the call today. Turns out we weren't the first choice, the other city in the running was recently featured in the news for unsavory goings-ons. The producer pulled the plug on that town and we got it by default. You'll want to get busy making up signs and what all."

"When is it?"

"Next week."

"Good heavens! How do they expect us to get ready in time?"

"The other town had a six-month warning. Still, we managed Gen Con. We can do this."

The thought of a bake-off in her town had her mind racing. She tapped her temple with her index finger. "As I recall, the stinkpot of a commissioner had you busy all during Gen Con doing stupid things such as watching empty parking lots."

"True. But he's gone. I'll be able to help you more. You can call on your Mother and your sister-in-law Maria to help. And you got

Ten."

"That's right," Ten enthused. "What else do you need?"

"Recipes," Donna muttered, stood, and moved as if in a trance toward the kitchen. She skirted around her husband in the process.

Mark followed. "I don't get it. I thought you'd be excited. You'll be able to attend the actual bake-off taping."

"Of course, I will." She smiled. Her husband, despite being a very successful detective, often missed the obvious when it came to her. "I'll not only be one of the contestants, I'll also win. I might want to practice acting gracious and modest, but only after I decide on my recipes."

"I agree you're a great cook. If anyone tasted some of the tempting spreads you provide for the guests you would be a shoo-in. I imagine this show has been in the works for a while. They pick out the contestants carefully. There might even be some celebrity chefs in the bunch."

"There won't be." She folded her arms and hoisted an eyebrow. "Have you ever really watched the show?"

"I've been in the same room while it was on, but there was so much chatter about ingredients or the inability to get certain ingredients that I tuned it out. Too much drama for me."

Aha! That explained all those odd answers he'd given her when the show was on. If she'd asked if a certain contestant deserved to win, he'd say she would if she made the best cake, showing he had not heard a word of her backstory. "If..." she emphasized the word, "you paid attention, you would know the show is about ordinary people making their best dish for the judges. Everyone has something they do very well."

"Yeah," Mark agreed. "My specialty is picking up a bucket of chicken on the way home."

The interior door swung open just in time for Tennyson to hear the remark. "Good one. My special dish is ordering pizza." Both men laughed as if it was the funniest thing ever said, but Donna didn't even chuckle.

"You two don't cook. Those who do have a dish they are asked to make for parties and get-togethers because they do it so well. The person tries different variations over the years until he or she gets the current version right. The dish is part of who they are. People identify them by it. It's Patty who makes the delicious potato salad. Ida, who makes the icebox cake or Norma, who always brings the tired green bean casserole."

With a shrug of his thin shoulders, Tennyson said, "I wouldn't want to be associated with potato salad or green beans. Besides, the bake-offs don't give away any money. Why would you want to win, anyhow?"

Instead of waiting for a reply, he ambled off leaving Donna and Mark alone in the kitchen. "If he would have stayed, I could have explained that I would have bragging rights. Being a bake-off winner would always be part of who *I* am. Maria could put it in the inn advertising. It could be on my resume, even my obituary."

"You're writing your own obituary?"

"All the smart people do. It's not smart to rely on relatives at such a time. Makes it easier on everyone. I'll pick out a photo, too."

Mark pressed a hand up against his heart. "Geesh. Do you have to talk about this?"

"No. Are you hungry?"

He chuckled. "That's right up there with asking me if I want coffee."

Donna bustled around the kitchen filling up the coffee pot and adding decaf due to the lateness of the hour. It wouldn't take her long to whip up a snack for her sweetie. Most wives might insist he fix it himself. She could, but he had suffered through the meeting for her. The least she could do was make him a snack. Besides, he never knew which items she had made for the inn and what was okay to eat. She'd learn that lesson a few months back when she told him to help himself.

"Okay. The lasagna roll-ups will be done in about ten minutes. The coffee, sooner. So, what do you know about the contestants?"

"Nothing. I assume the show brings them. Legacy's job is to keep the town commons looking green and picturesque. I wouldn't be surprised if the inn isn't booked solid. All the production crew will need somewhere to stay."

Well aware she had two couples both celebrating anniversaries coming in next week, she contemplated if there was a way of adjusting the dates of their visit to accommodate the production crew. Since anniversaries only happened once a year, she couldn't think of anything. What she wouldn't give to be in the bake-off. "Mark. Are you absolutely sure they have all their contestants?"

"Absolutely. What would the show be without contestants? Give it a break. You can have bragging rights in your next Christmas newsletter to all the cousins who aren't fortunate to live in Legacy."

She rested her hands behind her on the kitchen island and sighed. "I'd love to be a contestant."

Mark made his way to the coffee maker with an empty cup to await the fragrant brew. "I almost wish I hadn't told you. Although, Janice would have."

The cellphone chimed. Donna withdrew it from her pocket and swiped to the right. "Hello, Janice. Mark mentioned that you might call."

"He probably thought I would call about Alastair winning. Someone must have bribed the judges. I hear the man has money."

Donna agreed while her friend tore into the latest winner. She waited to spring the news about the bake-off. Janice must not know or she would have led with it. When a pause occurred, Donna jumped in. "Did you hear about Legacy hosting a bake-off?"

"Not that old county-fair thing. Lou Ella always wins with her brownie pecan pie. It's so sinfully good there's never any left to display with the ribbon since the judges eat it all—every year."

"No, it's a real bake-off. A television show. They are filming it here in Legacy. I guess there's more than one show. The crew is coming here next week."

"What!" Janice shouted the word forcing Donna to hold the phone away from her while grimacing.

"Mark heard it at the Chamber of Commerce meeting. Apparently, we were the runner up. Because you-know-who had a PR problem lately."

"I'm glad. Not about their PR problem, but that we snagged it. Tourism has been down with all the talk of red tide and hurricanes. I could use more people in my restaurant. I don't think people even bother to call and see if we have red tide. They assume all coastal areas are to be avoided. Not sure if the tourists are headed for the mountains or overseas."

"Hard to say. All I know is I want to be a contestant."

"Of course, you would. But I'm not sure if that's a good thing. After I got featured on the Food Channel, my business was good for a year. I mentioned the Food Channel on the menus, in the advertising, and even put up a big framed picture of me and the show's host on the wall. Didn't change any of my recipes, but I started hearing guests say they didn't think my chowder was Food Channel worthy. Before, it was delicious comfort food. I have no clue what these food snobs expect. Do you want that?"

"You know me better than that. Mark tells me all the contestants are already chosen. The only chance I have is if one of them drops *dead.*"

As soon as she said the word, she knocked twice on the wooden island causing her sweetie to give her a peculiar look in the midst of pouring his coffee. A sinking feeling came over her. The last thing Legacy needed was another inconvenient death, especially if it was murder.

Coming in March 2019

Author Notes

A Bark in The Night (the first book in The Talking Dog Detective Agency) was written after many requests from the local readers for a story set in Indianapolis. I certainly knew the town and surrounding areas. Many of the businesses and streets mentioned in the story do exist. The characters and the very lovable Max are entirely my creation.

Come and visit Indianapolis some time. You might be surprised at its several first-class restaurants and venues. I even have an adorable bed and breakfast to recommend too, The Nestle Inn.

Love to see you. In the meantime, stay in touch via my newsletter. Sign up at www.morgankwyatt.com.

Subscribers find out about exclusive freebies, contests, and personal appearances.

If you feel like writing a review, please do.

Reading takes you to your happy place.
MK Scott
www.morgankwyatt.com

CPSIA information can be obtained
at www.ICGtesting.com
Printed in the USA
LVHW081425230719
625012LV00025B/380/P